DIARY OF A LONELY GIRL: CLAIRE

By
K. Wiley Sider

ISBN: 0692794298
ISBN 13: 9780692794296

ONE

So I ran away. To be honest, there really wasn't much to run away *from*. My life as I knew it was over. My former husband left because he wasn't in love with me anymore. He wasn't even in love with someone else. He just wasn't interested in being around me and left. I hated my job as a benefits specialist with the government. I spent the majority of my day in a dingy, windowless office, writing useless employee notices for people who ignored them until they had a problem that I wasn't qualified to fix. I didn't have any friends to speak of. I didn't even have a dog, so there wasn't any reason for me to stay. So I cashed out my 401(k) and cleaned out the bank account, then packed what little I wanted to take with me in my twelve-year-old compact sedan and headed west. I drove and drove and kept driving until my previously loyal little car crapped out on me in a town called Hester, Wyoming.

As far as towns go, it was OK. Like what you'd imagine small western towns might look like. Two-story buildings and a small business section with a stoplight or two surrounded by modest, but well-cared-for, homes that eventually spread out to wide-open ranchland. In the midsummer sun, everything looked fresh though the air was oddly cool. I was used to unbearable DC humidity, so the mildness was a little disconcerting, even if welcomed. The scenery was nice. Green everywhere and mountains off in the distance that were far away enough to look unreal, like a painting or really realistic set design.

Now, I'm not one to believe in kismet or divine intervention, but my car broke down right in front of a brown brick building with a For Sale sign in the window. The woman who had just placed it there was locking the front door when my car rolled to a stop at the curb. I got out and was getting ready to stare stupidly at my nonfunctioning engine when I noticed her watching me from the sidewalk.

She must have thought I was interested in the building because she plastered the biggest, cheesiest smile on her face and walked over with her hand out.

"Hi, I'm Trisha. Are you here to see the bar?"

To be honest, I was caught off guard. I shook her hand, then looked at the building behind her. I was still staring at it when I realized she was actually pulling me forward.

It was a two-story building of light, sand-colored brick with tall windows all across the front on both the first and second floors. Someone had painted the window trim and door black, which set off the brick nicely. A black sign hung over the door. I hadn't noticed it before, and when I read the name of the business, I had to laugh.

The real estate agent, Trisha, caught my look and chuckled with me, though her chuckle sounded more embarrassed.

"Yes, the previous owners called it the Barking Spider. I don't get it myself, but people really seem to like the name around here," she said, then pulled me to the door. "So it's just under two thousand square feet on the first level. It has a recently renovated kitchen, though the current owners don't serve much more than chicken wings and potato skins. The second level is a fully furnished two-bedroom, one-bath apartment you can use for either additional income or as your own personal living quarters. The annual income for the last couple of years has been running about thirty to forty thousand, but adding more of a menu could easily bump that up."

I followed her into the space, and I admit I immediately fell in love. Sure the air was stale and smelled of dust, and it was a little tacky with antlers and neon beer signs on the walls. But the bar that ran the length of the left wall was deep black with a shiny brass rail and black leather barstools lined up neatly along the front. Behind the bar were black shelves filled with glasses and bottles and backed by beautifully mottled mercury glass. Instead of booths, small black tables were scattered across the rest of the space. The walls were exposed brick, and an ancient jukebox sat in the corner.

I paid scant attention to Trisha as she chattered about the various features of the space, even going so far as to demonstrate the amazing efficiency of the light switch next to the kitchen door. She wasn't lying when she said the kitchen was new. It shined like no one had ever used it. In fact, the whole place was spotless. Old and well-loved but spotless.

I followed her up a set of stairs that ran from a small foyer in the corner of the bar's kitchen to the second floor, where she unlocked another black door that opened to a semifurnished apartment that smelled of stale air and clean dust. The apartment was long and narrow with a small living room that faced the street. A seriously dated kitchen sat behind it, followed by two bedrooms and a bathroom off a long hallway that ran the length of the building. It was spotless up here as well but definitely more on the shabby side. And not shabby chic, just old and on its last legs.

We went back downstairs and out the front door, where Trisha paused to give me her final pitch.

"The liquor license conveys, so you won't need to wait for that, and the owners are really motivated. Most likely you could probably get set up within a week or two," she said. "So, what do you think?" She looked so hopeful I didn't have the heart to tell her the only reason I was there was because my car broke down.

"How much?" I asked. *Why did I just ask that? Like I am really going to buy a bar.*

"The owners are asking eighty thousand, but they are willing to work with the buyer on things like closing costs and such..." She trailed off as I did the math in my head. I had a cashier's check in my purse for $137,000. If I bought the bar, I'd have roughly $57,000 left. Take off another $1,000 to fix my car or buy something used and I'd have $56,000 to my name.

"I'll take it."

TWO

Oh my God, what did I just do? I knew absolutely nothing about owning a bar. Sure, I loved to cook and could probably learn to mix a drink or two, but I was settling into a town I knew absolutely nothing about to run a business I knew even less about. I sat in Trish's office and stared at the papers I'd just signed. The local bank had been more than happy to get me set up, and Trish had the papers written up and ready by the time the sellers walked in to complete the sale. The Hannemans, a very lovely elderly couple, were selling so they could retire to warmer, dryer climes. Luckily, they had asked if the bartender and his younger sister who waitressed could stay on, and I quickly agreed. At least I would have someone who knew what they were doing.

"So this is exciting, isn't it?" Trisha asked after the Hannemans left, and I wasn't quite ready to agree. She handed me the keys, and I stumbled out into the bright of the day a bar owner and new resident of Hester, Wyoming. I'd been there just under three hours.

I was pretty sure I might have lost my mind.

I made my way back to the bar, thankful that the town was too small to get lost in. It was actually a very nice town. I'd always thought of Wyoming as flat, but the mountains in the distance proved that particular assumption wrong. I knew nothing about them, but they created a lovely backdrop to the old western feel of the town. None of the buildings were particularly tall, and none of them had been updated or modernized. I wondered if that was due to lack of money or a desire to preserve the original architecture.

I turned the corner to return to the bar and saw a young man leaning against the door of my new home, doing something on his cell phone. He wore faded skinny jeans rolled up to show darkly tanned ankles above his sand-colored Converse. His gray T-shirt clung tight to his clearly fit frame, and a beige knit cap covered his dark hair. With his carefully cultivated hipster looks, all he needed to do was grow out his beard a bit more and he'd fit right in pretty much anywhere in Brooklyn or Seattle.

He stood and smiled when I walked up, revealing perfectly straight white teeth that his parents must have dropped a small fortune on. I was glad I was too old to be smitten with him. Twenty years ago I would have been struck dumb in his presence. Now I was just grateful he existed.

"Mrs. Dodd?" he asked, and I nodded. "Hi, I'm Luthien. Luthien Ross? The Hannemans said you might be interested in keeping me on?"

"Hi, Luthien," I answered. "And yes, I'd be thrilled if you stayed on... and your sister, too, right?"

He nodded. "Yeah, Mairen. There's not a ton of work around here, so if we can stay to help you, that would be great," he said as I unlocked the door and stepped into the cool shade of the bar.

Luthien followed me in and immediately went to his home behind the bar as if by habit.

Of course I had to ask. "So which parent loved *The Lord of the Rings?*"

Luthien laughed. "Good for you. Most people don't know where our names come from. My dad. It's kind of his thing."

"I'm surprised you're not Aragorn and your sister Arwen," I joked. "Or maybe Elladin and Arwen would make more sense."

Luthien laughed again. "Right. So if it's OK with you, Mairen can come and help us get set up. She's just waiting for me to let her know if you still want her."

Oh my God, was I relieved. "Oh, I definitely still want her. Have her come now if she can."

"Cool." Luthien sent off a quick text, then put his phone aside. "So what do you want to do first?"

I sighed. "I'm going to be perfectly honest with you. I have absolutely no idea how to run a bar, but the first thing I know I want to do is take down those beer signs and all the antlers."

Luthien nodded. "Totally agree. That stuff gets really dusty, and it's a pain to clean. It's also a little too...theme-ey...if you know what I mean."

"Great." I was thrilled he agreed.

I went over to the first set of antlers and pulled them off the wall while Luthien fetched boxes from the back. He found a stepladder somewhere and made quick work of the beer signs while I boxed everything up. I was pulling aside an empty box when the door opened and a female twin of Luthien stepped in. She was as beautiful as her brother, though her hair was long while his was hidden underneath his cap. "Hi, you must be Mairen," I said and stepped forward to shake her hand.

"Thank you soooooo much for letting us stay," she said with a youthfulness that made me want to hug her. "I'd way rather be here than at home."

"What's at home?" I asked, then mentally kicked myself for sounding nosy and mom-ish. I didn't even have kids.

"Our parents run an apiary and organic foods farm," Luthien said from the stepladder. "They do honey and preserves, some olive oils and vinegars, too."

I'm pretty sure my eyebrows went up. "This is kind of great, actually. I was thinking I might create a more bistro-type menu, and that's exactly the kind of stuff I'll need."

Both Luthien and Mairen smiled. "Then you'll need to meet Mom and Dad," Mairen said.

"And Grayson Childs," Luthien added.

Mairen glanced at her brother, then nodded at me, her eyes wide.

"And who is Grayson Childs?" I asked.

"He has a farm just down the road from ours," Mairen answered. "He does fruits and vegetables, and he has goats so he'll have fresh cheese and butter, too."

Well, that was a relief. That was one thing I wouldn't have to worry about. The more obvious issue still loomed, though.

"So tell me the truth," I asked. "Did I make a huge mistake buying this place?"

I was so relieved when both kids shook their heads with certainty.

"This place could be awesome," Mairen said with sincerity. "We get a decent amount of tourists coming through here on their way to Yellowstone, and there's tons of locals who come in here year round. Winters are a little rough, but there's not a whole lot else within walking distance for the people who live near town. And the Hannemans added wireless last year so you could advertise this place like an Internet café if you wanted."

"And even when there's, like, fifty feet of snow outside, people will still come just to get out of the house," Luthien added.

Well, that was good to know. Mairen and I went out to unload my dead car and carry what little I owned up to the apartment, then returned to help Luthien with the rest of the bar décor. When we finished pulling all the beer signs and antlers down, the brick wall looked better, if a little naked. I considered what might work there given the fact that my style tended to run on the modern side. Ironic that I ended up in a western town where art seemed to be of the guns and antler variety.

"I'm not sure what you're thinking, but that wall would make a great space for local artists to show their work. I could hook that up for you," Luthien offered. It was a great suggestion.

"What kind of art are we talking about?" I assumed lots of landscapes and cowboys, then mentally kicked myself for being so judgmental.

"Well, there's no shortage of landscape artists around here," he replied with a knowing smile, "but there's some great portrait artists and a couple of surrealists. They'd jump at the chance to show their stuff on an actual wall and not just on the Internet."

Well, look at that, another problem solved.

"I think that's a great idea," I said. "So it'll be a few days before all the paperwork transfers over, so I won't be able to open up until next week. If you guys want to come by and help me get the bar and kitchen set up, that would be great. And by set up, I mean help me figure out how everything works."

Luthien and Mairen nodded, then left, promising to return. I locked the doors behind them, then went upstairs to my new home and started unpacking. When I was done, the apartment didn't exactly look better, but it was definitely more livable. After I put what little I had away, I fired up my computer to do some research on running a bar.

Of course, the Internet was a huge resource for information, but so much depended on the type of clientele I would get. I had originally assumed all I'd get would be old-timers who wanted cheap booze, but the Ross kids made me second-guess myself. I also discovered that I hadn't even bothered to check any of the equipment or if there was a sales-tracking register. I made a list of everything the Internet said I needed, then went back downstairs. I was thrilled to find I needn't have worried. If the list was correct, everything was in place to run a successful business. Satisfied, I went back upstairs and started planning a menu.

When I finally had an idea of what might work, I gave myself a break and wandered around the apartment. At some point, all the furniture would have to be replaced, but that could wait. Right now I needed things like dishes and sheets and towels. What the apartment had was old and smelled like dust. Even the ancient washer and dryer that stood stacked in a small closet off the kitchen required a good vinegar rinse to smell normal again. I kicked myself for leaving so much behind, then took a deep breath. This was a new start, even if an ill-advised one. I deserved new towels. I got back on the computer and looked for the closest Target, which turned out to be two hours away in Montana. So time to make do with what was on hand until I could deal with the car situation.

I paused in my cleaning to stare out my windows, worried at the silence outside. I heard a slight rumble in the distance that was hopefully a busload of tourists looking for a nice place to stop and have a beer or six. With my luck, it was a single truck driver hauling God knows what to God knows where and who was pretty unlikely to stop at a bistro-style bar.

I'll admit I was seriously worried. I'd done exactly zero due diligence in determining if this was a smart business move. I'd either made a lucky decision or a hasty one, and there was no way to know until I had the bar up and running again. I cursed my impulsiveness, then tried to push all second thoughts to the back of my head. It was a nice town. So far, the people I'd met were all very kind, and I had two great kids who wanted to help me and wanted me to succeed. If I kept telling myself that, eventually I'd have to believe it.

THREE

The next week seemed to fly by. I managed to find a mechanic who could fix my car, then offered to trade it for a more Wyoming-friendly truck, which was old as dirt but ran great. My trip to Target was long, but the scenery was so beautiful it made the drive worth it. Luthien and his sister didn't bail on me and actually returned with a young local artist whose hypercolorized Wyoming landscapes were actually quite interesting. Kind of like Andrew Wyeth on acid. He and Luthien hung the large, brilliantly hued paintings across the wall opposite the bar and the end result was extraordinary.

Mairen and I went through the kitchen and made list after list of what was there and what was needed while Luthien set up the order for the bar inventory, adding a decent selection of wines to the standard whiskey and vodka fare.

When I had a plan for our first menu, Mairen and I went to her parents' farm to stock up. The Ross parents looked nothing like the Ross kids, though it was easy to see the origins of the children's good looks. Beth Ross had their fine bone structure and height while Jim Ross had their coloring. They were immensely kind and a great resource for locally sourced products. I left there with enough olive oil and vinegar to dress a year's worth of salads.

Next, Mairen and I visited Grayson Childs's farm. As soon as we drove up, I knew I'd be visiting there a lot. Not only did he have an impressive farm stand of fruits and vegetables, the farm was home to several greenhouses that ensured year-round produce. Mairen and I were looking over the lettuce options when a tall, thin man exited one of the buildings. He strode over, and I admit I may have done a bit of a double take. He wasn't handsome, exactly, but he had the kind of face that you wanted to keep looking at. His eyes burned blue from his deeply tanned face. It looked like the sun had cracked him in all the right places, and though his expression was stern, I could tell he was a good person. At least the goats that streamed to the fence rails to follow him seemed to think so, and in my opinion, if animals like you, you must be pretty decent.

"Mairen," he rumbled in a voice that made me want to crawl into his lap like a kitten. I shook off the frission that ran over my body. What was wrong with me?

"Hi, Mr. Childs," Mairen replied. "This is Mrs. Dodd...I was telling you about her? We're here to pick up some stuff for the Spider."

I was absurdly self-conscious about the fact that strands of white striped my black ponytail and my face hadn't seen a tan in at least a decade. To be honest, neither had the rest of me, and I felt positively lumpy next to the beautiful Mairen.

"Pleasure," Grayson Childs rumbled. His gaze was intense, and I wondered if he was studying me because I was new or because I was old.

"Mine as well, Mr. Childs," I said with a smile and wondered when I had become so charming. My stomach was churning butter under his scrutiny.

"Call me Gray. Good to hear you're doing something healthy at the Spider," he said. "People around here need something better than fried chicken strips and beer."

"We're doing beef and kale salad and a chicken and white bean chili for the opening," Mairen chattered.

I was grateful to her for filling in the conversational gap for me. While she and Grayson Childs talked about seasonal greens, I loaded my basket with pretty much everything the stand had to offer. It even had a cooler of assorted flavors of goat cheeses and butters. Not knowing how many, or few, people were coming, I was conservative in my estimates.

"You're going to need at least twice that," Gray commented in his deep rumble. "I have more in the dairy. I'll bring it by the Spider, if you'd like."

I seriously doubted I would need twice of anything, but why not? The refrigerator at the bar was huge, and if no one came, I could drown my sorrows in artisanal cheese.

"That would be wonderful," I said in a voice that really didn't belong to me. "Thank you so much."

Gray nodded, then started to walk away.

"Uh, Gray?" I called after him, as much to keep him there as to ask my question. "I need to pay you."

One side of Gray's lips went up in a small smile. "We can settle up later."

At that moment, whatever price he wanted, I was willing to pay. *Good grief, somebody spray me with a hose.*

By the time we got back to the Spider—as I guess most people referred to it—it was time for me to put Grayson Childs out of my head and start cooking. Since it was Thursday, I was planning a soft open just to see what issues might come up before we had the official opening on Friday. I'd decided to limit daily menu options to two entrees with a couple of sides. I would include freshly baked bread, which I was pretty good at making, and Grayson Childs's cheese. Of course I had to try it as soon as we got back to the bar, and it was amazing. He dropped off an entire cooler of it but left before I could pretend I knew how to flirt.

Disappointed but determined, I had massive pots of chili simmering and as much of the kale and mixed greens salad preprepped as I dared. The beef I'd have to make to order.

Pretty much everything was ready, so I was rolling out pie dough to do an easy blackberry galette for dessert. I figured I could prepare enough in advance to not have to worry about it later, and they were small enough that I could make more if we had a run on them. I just hoped the townsfolk didn't mind such limited options.

I'll admit I was incredibly nervous when Luthien unlocked the door at five. I could tell through the windows that there wasn't anyone on the street just waiting to come in. With the doors open and Mairen standing by, Luthien took his place behind the bar, and we all waited. And waited. And waited. Thirty seconds later I couldn't stand it anymore and went into the kitchen to cry into my chili.

I was contemplating how much chili I could eat in a week when Mairen walked in and placed a ticket in the first clip on the order shelf, then gave me a big smile.

I stared at the ticket, then stared at her.

"We have a customer?" I asked. Dumb, I know, but I was shocked.

"We have four," Mairen replied, then left the kitchen with a basket of bread. I read over the ticket and, numb, started plating. She returned a moment later with another ticket.

"Seriously?" I asked her, and she smiled.

"Seriously."

I stepped to the door to the bar and peeked out. Oh. My. God. People were coming. They were actually coming. And there were people sitting at the bar, waiting for Luthien to serve them their drink orders.

OK, so of course Luthien and Mairen's parents were here. That was really nice of them. I'd have to make sure to thank them for my dressing ingredients. And Trish came in with a man who was either a date or her husband. Also very nice. But behind her were people I'd never seen before, which was both thrilling and terrifying.

I stepped back into the kitchen and set up trays for Mairen to pick up as soon as she returned, which was only a moment later.

"Yay!" she squealed, then dropped off three more tickets and picked up her first tray.

"Yay!" I squealed to myself, then got to work.

For three solid hours, I busted my ass to get food out the door. Business was steady until after seven when people started coming in less for food and more for alcohol, which was fine with me. I'd prepped a bunch of quick and easy bar fare like thick-cut potato slices with crème fraiche and dill and turkey meatballs with cranberry chutney. When even bar food orders slowed, I went out to see what our crowd looked like.

Of course I was thrilled that the Spider was packed. I stepped behind the bar to find a smiling Luthien.

"We're doing great!" he said, and I marveled at how happy he and Mairen seemed to be for me. "People really seemed to like the wine options, too."

For that I was grateful. I'd made a small investment in the wine collection. Nothing too expensive but enough that it would be a financial hit if people weren't interested.

I was helping Lucien pour out a tray of French Malbec when the door opened and quite possibly the most handsome man I'd ever seen in person stepped in.

My God. He looked like a movie star with his perfectly windblown black hair and dark eyes. He was tall and clearly well-muscled under his crisp white button-down, and his jeans hugged the rest of him quite nicely.

"Yeah, that's Jeff Smallings," Luthien answered, then resumed chopping limes. I didn't realize I'd spoken aloud. God, how embarrassing but interesting that Luthien sounded less than enthusiastic about the presence of such male beauty.

"I take it you don't like him?" I asked, and Luthien shrugged.

"It's not that," he answered. "I guess I just don't get him."

"What do you mean?"

Luthien paused his knife and seemed to think about it. "Most people who come in here are really nice. It's a really good community. Mr. Smallings seems to be here because he can be a big duck in a really small pond. Like anywhere else he wouldn't be such a big deal and he wouldn't like that."

Huh, interesting. I watched Jeff Smallings work the room like a politician and thought Luthien maybe had a point. He acted more like the bar owner than I did, which was a little annoying. He took a seat at the end of the bar near a group of women and seemed to be holding court over them. I went over to take his order but really wanted to hear what he was saying to them.

"...so I heard *you* bought the Spider," one of the women said, and Jeff Smallings laughed.

"What makes you think I didn't? Oh, I thought about it, of course," he said conspiratorially, "but someone beat me to it."

"Yeah, *I* did," I blurted. So of course it sounded kind of shitty, but seriously, who did this guy think he was?

"So here's our new owner!" he crowed, and the women laughed like it was the funniest thing they'd ever heard. "Jeff Smallings," he said, then held out his hand. I shook it for a millisecond, then dropped it.

"What can I get you?" I asked with very little enthusiasm.

"Oh, I have a usual here," he answered with a wink to the women.

Of course they all tittered again.

"Which would be what, exactly?" Wow, I was being extremely ungracious, but this guy was a dick.

Luckily, Luthien stepped up. "Here you go, Mr. Smallings," he said and dropped a sweating glass of brown something in front of the man.

"Good job, Luthien," Jeff Smallings answered, then seemed to settle in to chat with me. So I turned around and walked away.

"OK, I get it," I said when I reached Luthien.

"Yeah," Luthien intoned soberly, then went back to his limes.

With Luthien's help, I managed to get the hang of bartending fairly quickly. Really Luthien just gave me easy jobs like washing glasses and pouring wine. I did have the opportunity to watch him make drinks and appreciated how careful he was measuring the alcohol. High bar liquor was really expensive, and I'd read online that a lot of bars struggled because of a bartender's heavy hand.

Mairen was great, too. The girl really hustled, and there was not a single complaint about service. I wondered if the Rosses would let me adopt their kids.

I was making my rounds of the tables when Gray Childs walked in. He gave me a polite smile, then stepped over to the bar and took a seat.

OK, so the smile was really just to be polite. I got it. Not interested. Who could blame him? I was a forty-eight-year-old divorcee. Oh well. At least I could thank him for the cheese, which was what I did.

Luthien was setting a beer in front of him when I walked up.

"So it looks like your first day was a success," he rumbled. God, I loved that voice. I cursed my libido and smiled.

"I had a lot of help," I replied, and it was true. "If it weren't for Luthien and Mairen, I'd be dead in the water right now."

"Oh, I'm not so sure about that," Gray said, eyeing me. "You can take credit for the food. I heard it was good."

I was about to thank him when a cry rang out. "Grayson, my man."

Gray and I turned to see Jeff Smallings stride over with his hand out like he hadn't see Gray in a decade. I stepped away to let the two men talk. Luthien was setting up another tray, so I went over to help him.

"I don't know what that's about," he mumbled. "Smallings's farm is right across the road from Mr. Childs. I'm sure they see each other all the time."

"The guy really likes to put on a show," I murmured, and Luthien chuckled, then caught himself. I glanced up to see Jeff Smallings approaching.

"Is there something you need?" I asked him as Luthien moved away with the tray.

Jeff Smallings leaned on the bar and gave me a winning smile. "So since you're new here in town, I thought you might like to see some of the area, maybe get a nice dinner. I hear our local hotspot has a new owner."

Was he really asking me out to my own bar? I was confused. Was that like a thing? I hadn't been on a date in over twenty years. Was I supposed to cook for him because I owned the bar? He must have read the confusion on my face because his brow furrowed and he changed tactics.

"I'm not sure if you've seen Sheridan yet, but it's a nice city," he said, sounding more like a normal person. "Makes for a very nice drive."

"That's really kind of you, but I'm not sure I have the time right now...just getting the bar started and all. Maybe when things are settled for me?"

Jeff looked at me with uncertainty, then gave me a crooked smile. "I'm holding you to that then," he said as his former personality asserted itself. He shot me a finger gun, then wandered down the bar to see who else he could pester.

"That might be the first time a woman has turned that guy down," an old-timer a few seats away joked.

I smiled and moved down the bar to freshen his beer. "What do you mean?" I asked as I slid a fresh glass of beer in front of him.

"Thank you kindly," the gentleman said and downed about half the glass right then. "I'm just saying Mr. Smallings there gets a lot of attention from the ladies. And he's pretty happy to oblige, at least for a while. Lotta broken hearts and dashed expectations around here."

I wasn't really that interested in Mr. Smallings, so I held out my hand. "I'm Claire."

The old-timer coughed, wiped his hand on his flannel shirt, then gave my hand a hearty shake. "Nice to meet you, Miss Claire. I'm Teddy."

"Nice to meet you, Mr. Teddy. I'm glad you came in tonight."

Teddy smiled, revealing some gaps in his grin. A week ago, the snotty, East Coast me might have recommended a good dentist, but I was in Wyoming now, and the smile was kind and very much appreciated.

"Oh, you might be seeing some of me," he said shyly. "Not much else to do round here at nights 'cept enjoy a nice beer and some tunes from that juke over there."

I looked over in wonder at the silent jukebox in the corner. I'd forgotten all about it.

"Why isn't that on?" I asked, and Teddy chuckled.

"It don't have wine-drinking music on it," he warned, then laughed.

I laughed with him, then walked over to turn it on. It lit up like an arcade, and the vinyl on the top began spinning like it had made a selection just for me. I checked the music options and found a lot of Hank Williams Senior and Johnny Cash, which wasn't surprising. I was surprised to see Bob Dylan and Woody Guthrie in there as well. I let the record go and was pleasantly surprised to hear bluegrass blaring out of the speakers. I found the volume control toggle on the back and moved it to low so people could still hear one another.

"Well, that's right nice," Teddy said when I returned to the bar. "Now it's a party."

I freshened another beer for him, then moved down the bar to see if Gray needed anything.

"Teddy's a good guy," he rumbled, and I agreed. "That's nice what you did for him. Life's been rough for him lately, so I'm sure he appreciates a little kindness. There are some around here who don't seem to notice people like him."

I wondered if he was talking about Jeff Smallings or someone else. I watched the crowd and saw that though people were polite, they kept their distance from the old man, like bad luck was contagious. I also noticed that though most of the men in the room were either farm fit or running to fat, Teddy was rail thin, the sharp lines of his bones cutting angles under his brown, paper-thin skin. I glanced at Gray, then moved back in front of Teddy.

"Hey, Teddy," I said quietly. "I've got a bunch of leftover food from dinner. Can you help me out and take some off my hands? I don't want to be eating chili all week." I hoped I hadn't offended him, but Teddy's smile was huge.

"Well, if you need my help, I guess I can clear off a bit for you."

I nodded, then went into the kitchen. I really did have some left over, so I made a huge bowl of chili and warmed a loaf of bread, then carried it out to set it in front of Teddy, who dug in like he hadn't eaten in a while.

"Let me know if you want more. I've got plenty," I whispered, then moved back in front of Gray, who nodded approvingly.

"Thank you for doing that," he said, his stern expression softening.

I shrugged. "He really is doing me a favor. I can't exactly serve leftovers. Does he live near here?"

Gray's brow furrowed. "Kind of. He's got an old farm just outside of town. It's mostly scrub, not really farmable, and there's no oil under it, so he gets by doing what he can. You'll see him around town, picking scrap from Dumpsters to sell or doing odd jobs."

"I've got a bunch of beer signs and antlers he can have," I joked, and Gray chuckled.

"He's more likely to decorate with those than sell them, but I don't think he'll turn them down. If you want, I'll load them in my truck and drive them over to his place."

"That would be great." And I meant it. Maybe Grayson Childs didn't want to date me, but he would make a great friend.

I moved back over to where Teddy was wiping out his bowl with a hunk of bread.

"Ready for another?" I asked, and he nodded with enthusiasm. I took his bowl into the kitchen, refilled it, and grabbed a couple of the galettes. When I returned, Gray was sitting next to Teddy. They were in quiet conversation. Teddy looked up as I approached with his second helping.

"Mr. Childs here says you got some stuff you need me to take for you?" he asked, then dug in to his chili.

"Yes, I do," I answered. "I took down those beer signs and antlers, and I don't really know what to do with them. I just want to get rid of them, but it seems a shame to throw them in the trash."

"Oh, there's no need to do that," Teddy said after he finished his bite of food. "I gotta guy near Cody that'll take that kind of stuff. Sells it on the computer."

"Perfect. Gray said he'll drop it by for you," I said, and Gray nodded. "Let me know when you're ready to go. I've got a bunch of chili to send home with you."

I was about to move away when Teddy reached out and grabbed my hand.

"Thank you, Miss Claire," he said with humble sincerity. "You are most kind to a decrepit old man."

"I don't see a decrepit old anyone here, but you're welcome," I replied, then gave his hand a squeeze and moved down to Luthien.

"Teddy's a good guy," Luthien said quietly. "The Hannemans were the same way with him, giving him food and such. He'll leave money, too. Not enough to cover what he drinks, but that never mattered to them."

"Or to us," I replied. "We'll be doing the same." Luthien gave me a smile that lit up the room.

Several tables were leaving, so I played host and walked over to thank them for coming and help Mairen clear the tables. I was pleased to see others coming in to take over the tables for the evening. Mairen took drink orders while I bussed, then went into the kitchen to pour bowls of roasted chickpeas and white truffle popcorn. I filled a tray with bowls to drop off around to the tables, then set several on the bar for the patrons there. Gray took a bowl of chickpeas and grabbed a popcorn for Teddy.

"These are really good," Gray said, and I blushed. "I was getting ready to go, but now I've got to finish this bowl."

"Do you have to go so soon?" I really enjoyed having him there. He was a comforting presence.

Grayson nodded. "Goats get up early," he said by way of an answer, then popped the last of the chickpeas in his mouth. "Come on, Teddy. I'll give you a ride home."

"Wait," I said quickly, then ran into the kitchen. I'd found a bunch of plastic take-out containers, so I filled two with chili and one with the rest of the galettes, then took them back out. Teddy was standing near Gray, pulling a small wad of crumpled bills out of his pocket. He flattened three of them, then laid them carefully on the bar.

"You said you could take these for me, right?" I asked, then handed them over.

"Yes, ma'am," he said without looking me in the eye.

"Teddy?" I asked, then waited until he looked at me. "We'll see you tomorrow, right? It's our grand opening, and I really hope you come."

Teddy smiled and nodded, this time looking me straight in the eye, then followed Gray out the door.

I turned to see Jeff Smallings moving toward me. I slid Teddy's three dollars to Luthien, who took them wordlessly and moved over to the register.

"I notice you gave Teddy some food," Jeff said. "I hope he paid for it. He's a bit of a bar rat, looking for droppings."

Wow, that was offensive.

"Of course he did," I answered, then wondered why I bothered. It was none of Jeff's business what I did.

"I just don't want anyone to take advantage of you," he said, then smiled. I was ready to be angry, but the smile seemed sincere.

"It'll be fine," I said with finality and moved away to take a drink order at the other end of the bar.

By the time the evening was over, I was exhausted but happy. Luthien and Mairen were amazing. We had a steady crowd until closing, and no one died from my cooking. I sent the kids home, did a quick cleanup in the kitchen, then went upstairs and fell into bed.

FOUR

The next morning I awoke to sunlight streaming through my curtainless windows and a massive ache throughout my entire body. I hadn't worked so hard in a long time, and every muscle was bitching up a storm. I rolled myself out of bed and stood under a warm shower until the pain subsided. Eventually I ran out of hot water so I turned off the shower, wrapped myself in my old terry cloth robe, then padded into my kitchen to make some coffee.

When I was finally awake and dressed, I parked myself in front of the computer to plan the menu for my grand opening. I'll admit I was pretty proud of the previous night's result. I'd always loved cooking, even though my ex usually turned his nose up at anything that wasn't beef and potatoes. Now that he was out of the picture, I could experiment as much as I wanted, and the worst that could happen would be nobody showing up to eat. Well, that actually would be the worst thing, since that would put me out of business. I surfed my favorite recipe sites for ideas and bookmarked a bunch of options for future menus.

My plan for the opening night's dinner was goat cheese gnocchi with blistered tomatoes and lamb meatballs in a yogurt cucumber sauce. No one seemed to mind the limited menu, so it was definitely going to be my thing. I did increase the side options, adding parmesan fries and roasted brussel sprouts, which I could make tons of without a lot of work. Of course it necessitated another trip out to Gray's farm.

Mairen came in and parked herself at the bar to write out menus, so I drove to Gray's by myself. I was disappointed to see the farm stand manned by a young man and not Gray himself. I wondered if the boy was Gray's son, then realized I knew absolutely nothing about Gray.

"Hi," the boy called out as I stepped up. "Are you Miss Claire?"

I nodded, and he pulled a cooler out from under the stand.

"I'm Justin. Mr. Childs said you'll need this. Can I put it in the truck for you?"

"Uh, sure," I answered. "What's in it?

"Some cheese, butter, eggs...and stuff," he replied as he loaded the cooler into the back of my truck and secured it with a length of bungee that dangled from his pocket. I'd also brought back Gray's cooler and found a massive one in the kitchen and had stowed both in the back so I wasn't taking Gray's cooler every time. I had a lot more to get, though, so the extra space was most welcome.

"Mr. Childs said to take you through the greenhouses so you can get whatever else you need."

"Is Mr. Childs here?" I asked.

Justin shook his head. "He's at a livestock auction, picking up some Nubians and La Manchas."

I had no idea what that meant but assumed it meant goats. I followed Justin into the closest of the greenhouses and found the grape tomatoes I needed for my gnocchi and a bunch of brussel sprouts. Gray grew everything, and I wondered who did better business, him or the grocery store.

I was making my herb selections when Justin and I heard someone pull into the drive. We stepped out of the greenhouse to see Jeff Smallings climbing out of his truck.

"I thought I saw you over here," he called out, which was odd. His land might have been across the road, but his buildings were far off in the distance. Unless he'd been standing at the rail that marked off his property, the only way he could have seen me was if he'd been using binoculars.

Weird.

I put on a polite smile and walked over.

"Just getting some things for tonight," I said, then wondered why I needed to explain anything. Justin gave Jeff a look, then carried my produce over to my truck.

"Where's Gray?" Jeff asked. I was about to answer when another truck pulled in behind Jeff's, then turned and backed up to the fence opposite the produce stand. Gray stepped out and shot a look at Jeff, then turned to speak to an older, taller version of Justin. They boy nodded then turned away.

Gray walked over. "Did you find everything you need?" he asked, ignoring Jeff.

I nodded, then stopped and looked at him consideringly. "Do you know where I can get lamb?"

Gray nodded. "Burrell's over toward Cody. He supplies all the resorts and restaurants. I'll drive you over there in a sec. Chase and

I need to unload these mothers first." He turned and gave Jeff a nod. "Smallings," he said, then walked away.

What's up with that? I wondered, then gave a mental shrug. I glanced at Jeff who seemed at a loss about what to do with himself, and then I followed Gray over to the truck. Chase had opened a gate in the fence and lowered a ramp, then opened the rear of the truck where a half dozen or so goats milled noisily.

"Awwwww," I said, sounding like a ten-year-old. "They're so cute."

Gray and Chase chuckled while Justin looked at me affectionately.

"You can help," Gray said, then guided me to the bottom of the ramp just inside the fence. "Make sure they head into the middle and not crowd the bottom. We don't want any of them stumbling or getting trampled."

I took my place, then guided each goat into the pen as they were led down the ramp. I was in love. Goats are so friendly. They crowded around me, nosing my hands like needy dogs, so I gave them all scratches behind their ears, their bellies bumping the sides of my legs like balloons.

I was enjoying myself so much I didn't realize all the men were watching me. Gray and the boys were smiling while Jeff looked at me like I'd lost my mind.

"Sorry. They're just so sweet," I said as I exited the pen. Chase closed the gate behind me while Justin pulled up the ramps, then drove the truck around the barn and disappeared.

"We can take your truck to Burrell's," Gray said. "We'll pass by here on the way back so you can drop me off."

"OK," I replied, then handed him my keys. I wasn't sure about what to do with Jeff Smallings. He still stood there, staring at us like something was supposed to happen. Luckily, Gray took care of it.

"Did you needed something from me?" Gray asked. Jeff shook his head.

"I just drove over to see if Claire needed any help," he lied.

"Oh, thanks but I'm good," I said lightly. "See you later then."

I climbed into the passenger side of my truck as Gray got in behind the wheel. Just to be polite, I waved as we drove off, but Jeff just stared at us.

"What was that about?" I asked once we were out of sight of the farm.

"I think he can't figure you out," Gray said with a smirk.

"What does that mean?"

"It means he doesn't understand why you aren't falling all over yourself trying to get his attention," he answered as he piloted my old truck farther out into the country. "So why don't you like him?"

"Why don't *you* like him?" I challenged. It was clear by his actions that Gray was not a fan of Jeff Smallings.

"It's not that I don't like him...exactly. I just disagree with his position on a few things."

"Like?"

"Like he wants to bring fracking to the area because he has a reserve of shale gas under his land. He stands to make a lot of money if it gets approved."

"And you disagree." I knew absolutely nothing about fracking, but it sounded bad.

Gray's face turned grim. "Very much. Fracking releases carcinogens into the soil. The process requires an enormous amount of water, which could be put to better use. Then that water gets stored in wastewater cells, which can leak and poison the earth around them. And it destabilizes seismic faults. A lot of places where hydraulic fracking is common are now seeing earthquakes on a regular basis. I think any one of those reasons is enough to prohibit Smallings from raping his land."

I stared out at the beautiful country passing by and imagined it all poisoned.

"Sounds obvious, then," I murmured more to myself. It seemed like a no-brainer.

"You would think, but the only thing important to Smallings is money. He owns his land, but he doesn't do anything on it. He doesn't farm or ranch. He just sits there, waiting for the day when he can turn it over to some oil company and find another shale-rich property. He doesn't care what he leaves behind."

Considering what kind of a guy Jeff was, I suspected that was true, and then a thought occurred to me.

"If his land is shale rich, then so is yours, right? You're right next to each other."

Gray gave me a sidelong glance. "Yeah? Why?"

I shook my head. "No reason. I was just wondering if Jeff got permission to frack...Is it frack? Anyway, wouldn't he try to extract the shale gas from under your property, too? Like sideways? Can you frack sideways?"

Gray seemed to be considering what I said. We drove in silence for a long time, and then he slowed to a stop and turned to look at me. I looked back and wondered why we had stopped.

"Is something wrong?"

Gray shook his head, then turned down a driveway. "We're here."

The ranch was huge, with fenced fields of sheep all around. Gray drove up to the first set of buildings and parked near an old barn. A giant of a man was limping toward us as we got out. He was easily the biggest man I'd ever seen in person. There was something wrong with his knee, and he favored it with each step. I felt like finding him a chair and urging him to sit down.

"Gray!" he called out as we crossed the gravel lot to meet him. "Haven't seen you in forever. What brings you by?"

"Hey, Harold. This is Claire Dodd. She just bought the Spider from the Hannemans, and she's looking for some good lamb."

"Oh! Very nice to meet you then!" Harold shook my hand with great gusto. "I thought Gray here was bringing a date by. Well, come on then. Let's see what we can find for you."

Harold turned, led us to the closest building, and opened a heavy steel door with little effort. We stepped into a massive refrigerated room that was floor-to-ceiling stainless steel and meat.

"We keep all our butchered stock in here," he said. "We just finished an order for a guy in Jackson Hole, so you're in luck. How much do you think you need?"

I had to think about that. Lamb was expensive, and each dish might take as much as half a pound. It was our grand opening, and the Ross kids had been spreading the word around town.

"I'm thinking a hundred and fifty pounds?" I guessed. That would give me three hundred servings. If I didn't use all of it, I could do mini meatloaf the next day.

"Sounds good to me. We're looking at about five dollars a pound then."

Wow, I had been expecting three times that. I was about to agree when Gray stopped me.

"Come on, Harold, five a pound? You can do better than that for that much lamb. She's taking a hundred and fifty pounds not five."

I watched as Harold made a face at Gray, who made a big show of shaking his head at the insult.

"Fine, I'll go down to four fifty."

"Four and we're good," Gray countered. I watched the exchange like a tennis match.

Harold seemed to consider it, then caved. "Four then. You're robbing me, Gray. Robbing me."

Gray smiled, then turned to me, and I was reminded all over again how handsome he was.

"Thank you, Mr. Burrell," I said and handed over $600 in cash. I would need to charge at least five dollars a plate to break even. I had no idea what prices people were willing to pay. Oh well, at least I liked lamb. Teddy and I would be eating well if no one came tonight.

"You're welcome. Now Gray gets to load up for you as payback for that nasty bit of haggling."

Gray smiled and started carrying out my purchase as Harold regaled me with stories of Gray's first efforts with his goats. I was surprised to hear he was relatively new to farming. I'd assumed he'd lived there all his life.

Once the truck was loaded, Harold shook my hand, and the rest of me with it, then bid us farewell.

"Thank you for that," I said as we drove away.

"I knew Harold was going to upcharge you for being a stranger. That's why I offered to bring you rather than just tell you how to get here."

I nodded, then stared at his hands as they skillfully maneuvered my truck. They were deeply tanned and looked strong. Well, I guessed they would have to be strong, considering all the work they did. Speaking of work...

"How long have you lived here?" I asked. "Mr. Burrell made it sound like you haven't been here that long."

"To Harold, anyone whose great-grandparents weren't born here is practically a stranger," Gray said with not a little bit of sarcasm. "But to answer your question, I've lived here just under ten years."

"Where did you live before?"

"Maryland," he said. It was a short answer, and he didn't seem like he was interested in elaborating. Well, it was a decently long drive, and we had to talk about something.

"What did you do in Maryland?"

"I was an analyst for the NSA."

"Huh, I worked for the FDA. Small world."

"It is. You me and twelve million other federal employees," Gray joked.

"Ha ha," I replied with sarcasm. "What I mean is I also lived in Maryland, worked for the government, and ended up in Wyoming. So statistically unlikely." I finished my statement strong, then realized, as a previous analyst, he was probably a million times better with statistics than I was, so I hoped he humored me and didn't start to perform complex math problems in his head just to refute me.

"Ah." Gray didn't argue, but he didn't look like he agreed, either. Great, no math-based arguments but no witty repartee, either. We spent the rest of the trip back to his farm in silence. Dead silence, since my radio didn't work. Well, this wasn't awkward at all. Nope, not a bit. This was so enjoyable I hoped he drove the long way back.

When he finally pulled into his driveway, I realized I had been holding my breath and finally released it when he pulled to a stop. I was feeling a little light-headed, but I had a load of food in my truck that need a refrigerator, stat.

"Well, thanks for the help," I said, then got in and drove away. Of course I looked back to see Gray staring after me, Justin walking up to stand beside him. Good, I hoped he was as unsettled as I was.

When I got back to the Spider, I pulled around back and parked near the kitchen door. I was lugging in the smaller cooler when I found Luthien had a surprise for me.

"Hey, Miss Claire," Luthien called out as I dropped the cooler onto the prep counter. They had propped the kitchen door open so it was easy to see we had company. Sitting at the bar was a heavily tattooed young woman with gorgeous chocolate-brown eyes and a severe haircut.

"This is Priscilla," he introduced. "We thought she might be able to help you tonight."

I walked over and shook the girl's hand. She had about a half dozen piercings in her face, and I marveled once again at seeing someone so alternative in the land of goat farms and livestock auctions. Despite the buzz cut and metal, she was beautiful.

"Nice to meet you, Priscilla. Are you a chef?" I asked, and she nodded.

"Yeah, I was a sous chef in Philly when the restaurant I was working at closed," she answered, her voice low and rich with timbre for such a tiny girl. "I came back home to save up some cash to try to get my own thing going back east...and you can call me Priss." If there was ever a name that did not fit the person, it was hers.

I regarded the young woman in front of me. Last night hadn't been so bad, but I did have to work like a madwoman to get everyone served before they starved to death.

"I can't pay you much, at least not right now," I said. In fact, I had no idea how much a sous chef was paid. I'd need to Google that as soon as I got upstairs.

"No worries." Priss shrugged. "A couple bucks here and there is more than I'm earning right now."

"All right then. If you're flexible, maybe we can make this work."

Priss smiled. "Deal."

"Great. Well, we have a cooler full of ground lamb we need to get in here, so let's at least get that done."

Luthien and Priss helped me carry in the lamb, and then Priss and I looked over my purchases for the day. I gave her my ideas for the menu and was thrilled that she agreed. She even had a couple of suggestions that I thought would be great, so we got started prepping for our grand opening.

FIVE

Priss and I worked through the remainder of the day to get everything ready. By the time our grand opening rolled around, we were in great shape and hoping people would come to eat all the food we'd prepped. I stepped out of the kitchen right as Luthien was unlocking the doors.

And...no one. Again. Well, instead of agonizing over it, I went back into the kitchen to wait, since that had seemed to work the day before. Priss followed and leaned against the refrigerator with her arms crossed over her chest.

"So I hope you like lamb because you and I'll be eating a great deal of it in the next few days," I joked.

Priss snorted. "People will come," she reassured, "and any minute now."

"How can you be so sure?" I cursed my uncertainty, but yesterday could have been a fluke. Maybe my food hadn't been as great as I had thought and this whole spontaneous endeavor was doomed to be a disaster. I wasn't a trained chef. In fact, most of my menu ideas were nothing more than bastardized Pinterest recipes.

"Because there really isn't anywhere else to go around here. People would have to drive all the way to Cody to get any kind of variety."

I stared at Priss for a moment, then smiled at her candor. It was kind of true. I had wandered around town a bit earlier, and there were very few options for the discerning palate. Hester didn't even have a McDonald's.

We stood in silence for a while, then jumped when Mairen came through the door. She stopped and smiled uncertainly, and I noticed she wasn't handing over an order ticket.

"So we have our first customer for the grand opening..." she began, then stopped.

I stared at her, then stepped through the kitchen door. Seated at a table in the center of the room was our first customer of the evening. Teddy had cleaned up nicely. His plaid flannel shirt was pressed and tucked in, and his beard was trimmed and neat. He might not be a paying customer, but I was happy to see him.

"Teddy!" I cried. "You look great!" Teddy's smile was shy but pleased. "What can I get for you this evening?"

"Oh, I'll just wait until everyone else is done," he said without meeting my eyes.

"Nonsense," I said, then pulled one of Mairen's menus from the bar. "Just give your order to Mairen, and Priss and I will get it ready for you."

Teddy sat up when he heard me say Priss's name. "Priss is here?"

"I'm here, Uncle Teddy," Priss said from the kitchen door. With a sweet smile that mirrored her uncle's, Priss stepped over and gave Teddy a big hug.

"My goodness, girl, you look like a comic book," he said as he looked over the art on her arms, then gave her another hug.

Priss laughed and returned the hug. "Thanks. Well, I'd better get to work. Miss Claire's come up with a really good menu. You'll love it."

I was grateful to Priss for the compliment. I gave Teddy a smile, then followed Priss back into the kitchen.

"Thanks for letting him come in here," she said as soon as the door closed. "He's a good guy."

"You're welcome," I answered, "but I have to ask. Why is it such a big deal to let him come in?"

Priss's lips pressed into grim line. "Uncle Teddy's had it rough. He was just a regular guy for a really long time. Then when my aunt got sick, things kind of fell apart. He took care of her the best he could, but he just couldn't keep it together and started drinking to cope. When she died, the drinking got worse. He lost his job and almost lost his farm." Priss paused and sighed. "Then one night he was driving back from a honkytonk near Cody and went into the other lane and hit a car full of tourists on their way to Yellowstone. One of them died, and Teddy went to prison. Anyway, when he got out...well, most people just stay away from him. He still drinks a bit, but he never drives. My dad or Grayson Childs usually takes him wherever he needs to go. So I guess anyone being nice to him is a big deal."

I was speechless. I couldn't imagine bearing the burden of guilt for killing another person, even by accident. And though our contact had been brief, he didn't strike me as a bad person. Tragic, definitely, but not malevolent.

"Well, I'm not going to condemn someone for something they did to someone else. He paid for his mistake. Who am I to judge?"

Priss nodded in agreement, then turned to fire up the stove.

Teddy proved to be a good luck charm for me. We had no sooner served him when the door opened to let in our first dinner rush. Priss and I worked nonstop as the tables refilled hour after hour. By eight, things finally started to slow down, and I stepped out to see how we were doing. The bar was still full, but most of the diners were gone, leaving behind a decent amount of drinkers. Teddy had moved to the bar and sat alone. I was about to go over to him when the door opened and Gray walked in. I'll admit my heart skipped a beat. I didn't know what it was about him, but his presence did funny things to me. I hid in the doorway and watched him make his way to the seat next to Teddy. Satisfied that Teddy had company, I went back into the kitchen to get some nibbles for my drinkers. I filled bowls with salted zucchini chips and spicy lime salt popcorn and gave them to Priss to carry out to the tables. While she was gone, I tossed mixed nuts with a maple and red sauce dressing, then roasted them with some fresh rosemary and kosher salt. By the time Priss came back, I had my own trays done and carried them out. Mairen walked up just as I was about to distribute them among the tables.

"You know people keep asking me how much the snacks are," she said as she stacked bowls up her arm like a seasoned server. "Maybe you should start charging for them if people are willing to pay. They're already leaving money on the tables."

I thought about that as she turned away. I'd read that salty snacks increased drink orders, but it hadn't occurred to me to charge for them. They were pretty expensive, so maybe Mairen had a point, though I was certain that money they were leaving was meant to be a tip for her.

When I stepped behind the bar to ask Luthien if the Hannemans had ever charged for bar snacks, Gray answered my question without my even asking.

"Tomorrow you should add your bar snacks to your menu," he suggested. "You could easily charge four bucks a small bowl and eight for a large."

I stopped in front of him. "You think so?"

Gray nodded with Teddy following suit. "I know popcorn is cheap, but nuts aren't. You should at least be charging for those. The Hannemans charged for bags of chips. No one is going to balk for something so much better."

"I'll pay for mine," Teddy announced and pulled out a small wad of crumpled dollar bills. He carefully extracted four, diminishing the wad by half and laid them neatly in front of Luthien. Luthien glanced at me. I nodded, and he took Teddy's cash and placed one of the larger bowls of nuts in front of the older man.

"Those are pretty spicy," I said with a smile. "You're going to need something to wash them down." I filled his glass from the tap and placed it in front of him.

"So it looks like you've had another good night," Gray observed. He wasn't kidding. The bar was so full that people were standing with their drinks, waiting for a stool to open up.

I sighed. "I know it's the novelty of it, and it's inevitable that we'll slow down. I just hope I can get steady business so this whole effort isn't a huge waste of money."

Gray gave me a crooked smile, which made my knees go weak. He was about to speak when Jeff Smallings showed up at his shoulder.

"Looks like another good night," Jeff said with hearty clap on Gray's shoulder. Ugh, right when Gray was about to say something encouraging.

I needed to be polite, so I smiled. "It is. Can I get you something?" I asked. I still had no idea what Jeff's usual was.

Of course I needn't have bothered. Luthien had it ready and slid it in front of the stool on the other side of Gray. Unfortunately Jeff took it as a cue to sit down and looked as if he were ready to chat. As much as I wanted to bask in Gray's manliness, I wasn't in the mood for Jeff and his banal conversation, so I wandered over to where Luthien was making a batch of margaritas for a small but noisy group of women sitting near the jukebox.

He looked up and smiled as I approached.

"Can I help?" I asked, and he nodded.

"So here's our famous margarita recipe," he began, then handed me a lime.

I spent the next couple of minutes learning to make a simple margarita, which, in my former life, I loved to drink but always assumed was too hard to make. By the time the order was done, I had the recipe down and felt so confident about how good they were I was seriously considering scheduling a margarita night for the bar.

"So all you really need to know is the basic recipe, two ounces of white tequila, one ounce of orange liquor, a half tablespoon of simple syrup or agave, and one and a half limes." Luthien was in full lecture mode, and I was his willing student. "Now when someone wants a flavored margarita, like melon or some other fruit like strawberry or kiwi, a lot of places will use flavored syrup." Luthien pulled a face and looked like he might gag a little. "Those really aren't any better than the bottled mixes you can buy at the grocery store. In fact, flavored syrups usually taste worse." Luthien turned, reached into the small refrigerator behind him, and pulled out a container of pureed watermelon. "So let's pretend someone's ordered a watermelon margarita. If they order a pitcher, we can do that pretty easily with watermelon, but we usually get only single-glass orders."

I watched as Luthien got out his ingredients and stepped aside. I stared at him until I realized I was supposed to make the margarita so I stepped forward and stood as if ready to perform surgery on the high bar alcohol. Out of the corner of my eye, I could see Gray smiling at me as Jeff chatted, oblivious to the fact that his conversation mate wasn't paying a lick of attention to him.

"Now, first you're going to muddle the watermelon a bit with some sliced strawberry. You only need about a cup's worth so the drink isn't too sweet."

Luckily, I knew what muddling meant. I poured the watermelon into my glass, added some sliced strawberries, then grabbed the small wooden pestle and crushed the mixture until it resembled a mostly melted, but chunky, snow cone.

"Now you can go ahead and add your alcohols," Luthien instructed.

As ordered, I measured and poured out the tequila and orange liquor, and Luthien nodded in approval.

"Because watermelon has so much natural sugar in it, you really only need a little bit of syrup," he said.

I poured what looked like a teaspoon's worth, then glanced at Luthien, who judged it to be enough.

"Then a squeeze of lime and you're ready to shake."

I picked up one of the smaller limes, cut in in half, then squeezed it into my mix. I had to admit it smelled good, and the color was beautiful. I put the shaker cap on, then went crazy mixing my ingredients for the next ten seconds. When I opened the cap, the aroma of tequila-infused watermelon made me smile. Luthien slid a salt-rimmed glass over to me, and I poured my very first solo effort out.

It looked great and tasted even better. I wasn't a sweet drink kind of girl, but the lime and salt cut the sweetness of the watermelon nicely. My cook's brain started to think about what else could go into the drink.

"Now if you really want to make your drink pop, you can add things like basil or jalapeño to give it a little extra kick," Luthien said.

He'd read my mind, and I smiled. Just then one of the women Jeff had entertained the night before stepped up with her eye on my glass.

"I'd love one of those," she said.

At first I thought she was just being polite, but she was staring at the glass like it was her last meal before dying. Far be it for me to deny the poor woman one of my culinary masterpieces.

"Coming right up," I answered, then set about making another one. I strayed a little bit from the recipe and added a squeeze of orange and slices of strawberry, then slid it across the bar. I glanced at Luthien, who looked impressed. He smiled and nodded as the woman took a sip.

"Oh, it's really delicious," she exclaimed.

"Thank you," I answered and was about to move away when she spoke again.

"I'm Kim, by the way," she said and held out her hand. I reached over, shook it, and hoped my hand wasn't too sticky.

"Very nice to meet you," I said.

"Same here." She smiled. "I just wanted to tell you how good everything was. Your food is amazing."

I wasn't sure about amazing, but it was incredibly nice of her to say so, and I told her.

"I understand you're new to Hester," she continued, "so if you ever get a free moment, some of the other ladies in town and I have a book club that meets every week or so. You're welcome to join us. We're reading *The Silent Wife* right now. We just started, so you shouldn't have any trouble catching up...if you're interested."

I didn't know what to say. It was kind of her to extend the invitation, but it caught me off guard. I wasn't used to such kindness. People back east weren't always so gracious. In my old neighborhood, everyone just kept to themselves. I had barely known my next-door neighbors and hadn't even known they'd moved way until some random toddler wandered into my backyard followed by an equally random mother. Even then, neither said hello, just apologized and escaped to the safety of their own patch of grass.

"I'd love that," I answered. "Though I hope Amazon delivers out here, since I haven't come across any bookstores lately."

Kim smiled and waved my comment away. "Most of us use Kindles or iPads...or don't even bother reading the book and just drink wine while the ones who actually read the book talk about it," she answered, then indicated one of the women at the end of the bar. "Theresa there likes actual books, so she sets the reading list and orders everything ahead of time. And, yes, Amazon does deliver here."

"That sounds great. You all are welcome to meet here if you'd like."

Kim nodded, then picked up her drink. "I love that idea. I'm going to go let the other ladies know. I'll let you know when we all want to meet next, OK?"

I nodded, then watched her rejoin her friends.

Luthien moved beside me. "Just to let you know, those ladies tend to drink more than they read. My mom used to go to their meetings, and half the time they couldn't even remember what book they were supposed to be talking about."

I gave Luthien a wink. "Sounds like my kind of club."

Jeff Smallings had moved off to make his rounds among the patrons, so I stepped over to Gray to see if he needed anything. Really I just wanted to stand in front of him and bask in his masculinity, but he didn't need to know that.

"Looks like another good night," he said. I refilled his popcorn bowl and was gratified to see him take a handful.

"I know it won't stay like this. I just hope I can make a decent living once the novelty wears off." I reached up and brushed a strand of hair off my forehead, then despaired at the trail of salt I was certain I'd left behind.

"What brought you to Wyoming anyway?" Gray asked.

I shrugged. "Bad luck," I answered immediately, then regretted it. It came out sounding like an insult to the town and not at all what I meant.

Luckily, Gray laughed. "Really? How so?"

I took a deep breath, then let it out. "When my husband and I divorced, I felt like I didn't have any reason to stay in Maryland, so I packed up what I could and drove away. I made it as far as Hester when my car broke down in front of the Spider, and here I am."

Gray stared at me. "And so you decided to buy a bar? Just like that?"

My face burned with embarrassment. "I guess so. My ex told me I was boring...that I never wanted to do anything exciting. I guess I subconsciously wanted to prove him wrong. It sounds stupid when I say it out loud."

Gray shrugged. "No more stupid than buying a goat farm without knowing a single thing about goats. Thank God for the Internet."

I nodded in agreement. "Thank God for the Internet."

Gray chuckled, then picked up his glass and finished off his beer. He set the glass down on the bar, then clapped Teddy on the shoulder.

"Come on, buddy," he said. "I'll give you a ride home."

Teddy started like he'd been dozing, then slid off his stool. He paused to pull some cash out of his wallet, but Gray stopped him. "You already paid, Teddy. Right, Claire?"

Teddy stared at Gray, then turned his bleary gaze to me.

I nodded. "That's right, Teddy. You're paid up."

"G'night, Miss Claire," Teddy mumbled, then followed Gray out of the bar.

Mairen sidled over and leaned on the bar next to me. "I think Mr. Childs likes you," she said with a smile.

I gave her a look. What did she see that I didn't? "I'm old and boring, and I'm pretty sure he isn't even remotely interested in me."

Mairen's eyebrows went up. "You are not even old."

I cleared Gray's and Teddy's glasses and grabbed a wet bar towel to clean up.

"I could be your mother," I said without looking up. "Most men want some young, pretty thing like you. Not some dumpy old lady like me."

"Um, you're not exactly mom age," Mairen said, and I wanted to hug her.

"I'm absolutely mom age," I replied with regret. "I'm forty-eight, so I can easily be both your parents. What are you, twenty-two, twenty-three?"

Mairen laughed. "I'm twenty-two. Luthien's twenty-five."

"See?" I gestured at my decidedly mom-like body. "I'm definitely mom age."

"Well, you look an easy ten years younger, so you could totally lie about your age and no one would know," Mairen said wisely. "Besides, Mr. Smallings totally has the hots for you."

I laughed and looked over at Jeff Smallings, who happened to glance over right at that moment and raised his glass as if in a toast.

"I think he has the hots for just about everybody, but thanks."

Mairen shook her head at me like I was crazy, then went to service her tables. Maybe I was crazy, but I knew I wasn't wrong. I was at least ten years past my dating expiration date, and nothing was going to change that. And whatever hots Jeff Smallings might have for me was nothing more than an instinct to command the attention of whoever happened to be around him. It didn't have anything to do with me personally.

I fell into a bit of a funk and spent the rest of the evening trying to pull myself out of it.

SIX

I wasn't wrong when I said things would slow down after the novelty wore off. Though we didn't have nearly as much as our first two nights, business remained somewhat steady but down enough that I decided to open for lunch. Priss was a master at sandwiches, so our day business grew even if the nights dropped a bit.

Mairen wanted to be a blogger and was a natural at marketing, so she took on the task of promoting the Spider as a premier stopping place for tourists traveling through to Yellowstone. Hester was technically located in the Big Horn Basin as it sat between Yellowstone and the Big Horn Mountains. Lots of people drove through on their way west to either Yellowstone or Jackson Hole and needed a place to eat so Mairen's efforts ended paying off for us big time. In fact, we were doing well enough that I was able to pay Priss an actual salary.

After my first month, I felt like I was getting into a good groove when the weather began to change. Nothing too serious but a series of storms had been through and the rain was really killing it for me.

At least I had Jeff Smallings to keep me afloat. That was actually kind of a joke. He came in as much as Teddy did and ironically spent about as much, too. He never ate and nursed the same drink for the entire night but always managed to look like the life of the party.

He'd increased his efforts with me as well and that was getting seriously annoying. With Gray coming in less, Jeff would make his rounds of the tables, then park himself at the bar and pester me all night long.

At first I tried telling myself that at least someone was interested in me, but my God, for as much as the man talked, he had very little to say. It was like listening to a politician answer an uncomfortable question for four hours straight. If it weren't for the weekly book club, I would have been seriously suffering for meaningful adult conversation.

I was deeply grateful for the book club. I loved having the ladies at the bar, even if I couldn't spend the whole time with them. They paid their way, which was great, since they drank like fish and they were a lively group. Kim, who'd originally invited me, was incredibly sweet, and the others were equally nice. The life of the party was Margaret, who had a wicked sense of humor and shared my dislike of Jeff Smallings. Her husband was an environmental lawyer who had spent the last couple of years blocking Jeff's efforts to introduce fracking to the area. Her rants were the stuff of legends, and she drank so much I think her bar tab alone kept me in the black my first month.

They had made Thursdays their regular night, so I decided to prepare a special dinner for our first-month anniversary. I was going to do goat cheese and rosemary biscuits with grilled chicken and gravy, which necessitated a trip out to Gray's. He hadn't been in as much, which hurt my feelings until Luthien mentioned something about goats hating storms. I didn't want to admit it, but I was really looking forward to seeing him, even if it was just to enjoy the deep rumbling of his voice.

Priss and I loaded the coolers into the truck, and I set off for the farm while she stayed behind to get some prep done. The morning had started off sunny, but by noon, the sun was gone, and the sky had turned a stormy gray. The clouds off in the distance were stained with blacks and grays like a painting, which turned the landscape a deep, saturated green. Rain was coming, but it looked far enough away that I should have plenty of time to make it to Gray's and back.

Justin was just closing up the farm stand when I drove up.

"Hey, Miss Claire," he said with a wave as I got out of my truck. "I moved everything inside, since the storm is coming. I'll get you loaded up. Then I've got to get home before the rain comes. These roads tend to wash out."

I nodded, then followed Justin into the small barn near the farm stand with my list. Admittedly I was disappointed not to see Gray but too embarrassed to ask after him.

Justin took my list, then left me to load everything onto my truck. I carried what I could, then let the strong young man to do the heavy lifting. I stood just under the eaves of the barn and watched the clouds roll over the hills toward the farm. The rain had started, and the front of my jeans were already soaked.

"You're good to go. Make sure you get back to town fast. Rain's coming," Justin called, then set off at a jog toward his own truck.

"Thanks, Justin," I called after him, and he waved.

As I pulled out onto the road, the sky opened up, and it began to pour buckets. Justin wasn't kidding. In minutes the road had turned into a river, and I wondered if my truck was tall enough to avoid the water flooding the engine. I was cursing my luck and trying to peer through the side-slanting rain at the road in front of me when my truck suddenly fishtailed to the right with such severity the seat slid beneath me and my body slammed into the door.

I let the truck come to a complete stop and took stock of my situation. It was not great. The bed of my truck had dropped so much on my side that the coolers had slid down to the tailgate. My left arm and shoulder hurt so badly I hoped I hadn't broken anything, and I was pretty sure when I got out I was going to find I had a flat. So I got out.

Yup. I had a flat. I stood in the shin deep water and stared at the tire that was so flat the rim rested, half-underwater, on the road itself.

Luckily, I knew how to change a tire. Unluckily, the spare was mounted under the bed of the truck, which was partially submerged in the river that used to be the road.

I opened the toolbox just behind the cab and pulled out a tire iron. I was soaked and sore and shivering but determined to get that tire off. But with the rain, it just wasn't going to happen.

I was still struggling with the lug nuts on the tire, my fingers aching and my teeth chattering, when a pair of lights trailed across the back of my truck. I turned to see Gray climbing out of his own truck with Jeff off in the distance, coming up behind him. Jeff looked soaked, like he'd walked across his property.

"Leave it, Claire," Gray rumbled, then took the tire iron out of my numb fingers and tossed it into the bed of my truck. "The road's washed out ahead. You won't make it back."

I was too cold to answer, so I just nodded. Gray led me back to his truck, pulled out an old barn coat, and wrapped it around me, then lifted me in behind the wheel. I slid over as best I could and waited for him to get in. When he didn't, I turned to see Jeff had walked up.

"I've got her," Gray said, and he sounded annoyed. If I hadn't been so cold, I would have gotten out and just waited out the rain in my own truck. The last thing I needed was to be a burden to someone.

"I can take her," I heard Jeff say, and Gray answered with what sounded like a snort.

"What are you going to do, carry her to your farm?" Gray said, then got in the truck and slammed the door without waiting for an answer. By the time he got turned around, it was raining sideways and Jeff Smallings had already turned for the hike back to his farm.

"Idiot," Gray muttered under his breath. I didn't necessarily disagree, but his earlier annoyance still stung.

I despaired for my poor truck left in the middle of the road and hoped no one hit it.

"No one is dumb enough to go down that road until the storms pass," Gray answered. I hadn't realized I'd spoken out loud.

Great, now I'm dumb, too. If I hadn't been so cold and sore, I would have opened the door and thrown myself out of the truck just to get away from his scorn. I'd spent the last five years of my marriage living with a man who treated everything about me with contempt. I wasn't about to allow it for another five minutes. I flexed my hand to get it working again, but it felt like a block of ice. By the time I'd worked it enough to open the door, we were back at Gray's farm.

I wanted to tell him to take me back to my truck, but he'd gotten out and was coming around to open my door. I was about to speak when he lifted me from the seat and carried me into the house. The sudden change to warmth set my skin to tingling. It was almost as painful as my shivering. Gray set me down on a worn but soft brown sofa in front of an old stone fireplace where flames were just starting to lick at the blocks of wood placed there. My clothes were soaked and still felt cold despite the coat.

"You'll freeze in those," he said as if reading my mind, then knelt in front of me and began unbuttoning my shirt.

"I can do it," I snapped, but my fingers weren't thawed enough to work the buttons. Gray waited patiently while I fumbled, then gently moved my hands aside and resumed undressing me.

I'd been fantasizing about this moment for a month, yet the moment was quite possibly the least sexy moment I had ever had in my life. Gray was clinical in his undressing, even when he peeled my rain-soaked jeans down my legs. He pulled a lap blanket over me, then carried off my clothes. I pulled the blanket closer, but I just couldn't get warm. Gray returned to hand me a steaming mug of tea for which I was sincerely grateful. I tried to steady my hands around the warm mug as he wrapped another soft, thick blanket around me, but I was freezing to my core and couldn't stop shivering. He held the mug as I tried to take a sip, then placed the mug on the table in front of us. He moved beside me, wrapped his long arms around me, and pulled me to his chest. Knowing how annoyed he was with me, it was weirdly both comforting and uncomfortable. I closed my eyes and buried my face in the soft flannel of his shirt. He smelled like a combination of leather, sweet skin, and goat. I felt him rest his chin on my head, which helped with the tremors.

Then the next thing I knew, I was waking to a sense of watchfulness. I must have slept, for my eyes still felt heavy. Gray's legs were under me, but my face rested on the soft fabric of the couch and not Gray's chest. I heard the rain hammering against the roof of the house, and I mourned my poor truck. I lifted my head to look out the window but saw Gray watching me with an uncomfortable intensity. His face was so close I could have stuck out my tongue and licked the end of his nose. Instead he moved closer and pressed his lips gently against mine. They were warm and soft but firm and tasted like the tea that sat in front of me. He pulled back for a second, and my own lips missed his warmth.

Gray stared at me as if waiting for some objection, then leaned over and kissed me again. This time for longer and with an urgency I shared. As his lips moved over mine, I felt his hand move up and cup my breast, warming it despite the damp of my bra. I must have moaned, and it must have sounded encouraging because Gray slipped his fingers under my strap and pulled my bra down to expose my breast. Another moan must have escaped as Gray's hand covered my now bare breast, his thumb grazing my nipple with deliberate slowness. It stiffened under his touch, and my breath caught under his lips. Gray paused for a moment as if making a decision, then picked me up, blankets and all, and carried me into his bedroom. I was so hungry for his lips that I wasn't aware his clothes had disappeared until I felt the warmth of his skin against mine. Soon both my bra and panties were gone as well, and we lay, skin to skin, the length of his body setting mine on fire.

His lips explored the contours of mine until mine opened and his tongue gently tickled the delicate skin just inside. My body ached to feel all of his. I needed him to be so close that we were one being, with no break between where mine ended and his began. I needed him inside me, and as his hand moved from my breast to the cleft between my legs, I knew he shared my need. My moans turned to cries as his fingers moved over my clitoris, then into me as if testing my readiness. He needn't have worried. I had been ready for him a month ago. His thumb continued to work my clit until tremors ran through me. Then at the crest of my orgasm, he pushed into me, his full length filling me, stretching me with a delicious explosion of pleasure. I cried out as my orgasm peaked, and he moved more urgently inside me, then cried out with his own pleasure. While still inside me, he gently lowered his body next to me, the bare brown of his chest rising rapidly from his exertions. After a moment he pulled the blanket over us and gathered me in his arms, and together, we slept.

When I awoke again, the rain had stopped, and outside the window, a night sky shone with stars. Gray's arms were wrapped around me, his chest warming the skin of my back. I felt safe, protected, and never wanted to leave, but nature had something else in mind. I eased out from under his arm and grabbed the small blanket that had been pushed to the bottom of the bed. Wrapping it around my naked body, I made a guess and found a small bathroom just off the bedroom. With that taken care of, I washed my hands, then regarded myself in the mirror. The rain had done a number on my hair, and it haloed my head with mass of loose curls. My lips were swollen from Gray's kisses, and I looked like I'd been thoroughly fucked, which I had. Thinking Gray was still asleep, I crept back into the bedroom, but the bed was empty. I looked up to see Gray standing at the window, wearing a pair of faded jeans, his chest bare. Lightning lit up the window behind him, revealing his perfectly molded chest. Goats must provide a perfect exercise regimen; the man had not an ounce of fat on him.

"Storm is coming back," he said quietly. Through the window, I could see lightning carving stripes across the sky, lighting the angles of his face as he stared out at the night.

"I need to call the kids and let them know I'm stuck," I answered.

Gray turned to me. "I called them already. The Ross kids won't be able to get home, and I don't know where Priss is staying, but if she's at her parents, she might be stuck, too. They live out toward Big Horn. I told them to stay up in your apartment. You have two bedrooms, right?"

I nodded. I was glad he'd thought to keep them at the Spider. I'd have been devastated if something happened to the kids.

Gray glanced out the window as a flash lit up the sky and turned the night to day.

"If the thunder comes, I'll have to go out to the barn. The goats are afraid of the noise." Gray turned away from the window and moved to the door.

"I'll get us something to eat," he said, then nodded toward a chair that flanked a small dresser. "There's dry clothes there for you," he finished, then closed the door behind him.

Well, that hadn't been awkward at all. Nope, not one bit. Clearly a mad love affair was in our future, and I couldn't wait to hear him proclaim his deep and undying love for me. I stepped over to the chair and picked up the soft pink flannel shirt. And why did he have women's clothes? I was hesitant to wear another woman's clothes, but I was freezing, so I pulled on the shirt and and jeans and found both were so long on me that this other woman was clearly a giant or an NBA basketball player.

Fine, I was using humor to cope with the fact that I'd just slept with a man I'd been fantasizing about for a month and he'd just given me another woman's clothes to wear *and* left the room, worried about his goats. Definitely not the scenario I'd been envisioning. I was experiencing a crushing disappointment as I rolled the jeans up a dozen times so I could at least walk normally, then tried to distract myself by going back into Gray's bathroom to see if this mystery woman had any ponytail holders lying around. I opened the first drawer and yup, there was one and it was a light beige. She must have been a blonde. Fabulous, good to know Gray liked blondes. I pulled the mess of my mostly black hair up into a ponytail, then left the bathroom. Blonde giant probably had perfect ponytails. I was losing this contest fast, and I hadn't even met the woman yet.

I went into the kitchen where Gray was putting two small baking dishes into the oven.

"I hope you like eggs," he said, then poured more tea. I paused a second to gauge the emotional temperature of the room, then gave up and took a seat at the old wooden table in the center of the kitchen. The house was old but cool old, not bad-taste-grandma old. The kitchen had been updated at some point, and the appliances were brand new. The cabinets looked original, though they had been whitewashed at some point, as had the exposed brick backsplash. The counters were butcher block and were probably original or mostly original as well, but they had been stained a dark chocolate color. But no bad vintage wallpaper or homemade needlepoints here. Everything was spare and clean.

I watched as Gray got out forks, knives, and napkins and set the table as if company were coming. When the timer dinged, he pulled out the pair of baking dishes and set one in front of me. Gray had baked eggs with what tasted like ham, grape tomatoes, and spinach with a little garlic and some kind of cheese that wasn't goat cheese. Pecorino, maybe? It looked delicious, and when I tasted it, it was delicious. I was totally going to rip off this recipe.

"It's delicious," I said quietly. "Thank you."

Gray finished his fast and put his fork down, then sat back and looked at me. I squirmed inside, not because I was uncomfortable but because, my God, that man affected me in places I had thought were long dead.

"I'm sorry about...what happened," he said, then looked away, and my libido cooled immediately.

Wow, I had thought being ignored hurt but regret? That was a real killer.

I didn't know what to say, and he was looking back at me as if I were supposed to respond with a shared regret. Well, I didn't regret what happened so I tried to change the subject instead.

"So whose clothes are these?" I asked. "She must be really tall."

Gray looked toward the window as a distant rumble followed the sudden flash.

"My ex-wife's," he answered, then got up, took our empty plates to the sink, and moved to the door. "I've got to go out and check on the goats..." he started, and I nodded.

"They are afraid of thunder. I get it," I finished for him. Something about my tone must have satisfied him. Gray just nodded, then left the kitchen.

I sat in the chair and stared despondently at the mug of tea in front of me. I'd figured Gray for a coffee kind of guy, but really, what did I know about him? Very little, really. From the East Coast, worked for the government, divorced, liked goats, and felt sorry he slept with me. I was starting to get annoyed. Really annoyed. So annoyed that I decided to confront him right then and there. I got up and left the kitchen to make my way across the farmyard when a deafening crack split the night, stopping me short. Shit, no wonder goats hated storms. That had just scared the shit out of me.

I hurried across to the goat barn and let myself in through the small, human-size door. The lights were on, but judging from the way they were flickering, probably not for long. Gray stood in the center of the pen, surrounded by goats bleating their fear. He was making soothing shushing noises and petting as many of them as he could. I made my way over, then climbed over the rail that kept them penned. As soon as I stepped down, they clustered around me, and their cries were heartbreaking. I reached for the closest ones and tried to comfort them as best I could, but each crack of thunder startled me as much as it did them.

"Claire," Gray called out. "There's a radio in the office behind you. Can you bring it out and turn it on? It might help."

I nodded, then turned and climbed out of the pen. I made my way into the office and found an old clock radio tucked in the corner of an even older desk. I carried it to the doorway as far as its cord would allow, then turned it on. It was already set to a classical music station, which was pretty remarkable, since most radio stations in the area played country music. I turned it up as loud as I thought reasonable then settle back in amongst the shivering goats.

Gray nodded his approval, and together we sat in the pen with the goats and soothed them. It was kind of cool how the goats settled down around us and with the music and the sound of rain on the roof; their soft slow breathing was enough to calm my earlier annoyance. Mostly kids surrounded me while Gray had the nursing mothers clustered around him. I loved their sweet sleeping faces and caressed each in turn so that no one felt left out. They were so precious I didn't want to leave them, even as the storm moved off. I looked up to see Gray watching me.

"They're fine now," he said, then stood, careful not to disturb the animals closest to him. I did the same. "We can go."

I climbed over the rail and left the barn with Gray behind me. I had made it halfway across the farmyard when Gray caught me and pulled me close.

"God, you are so beautiful," he whispered, and my heart soared.

He pulled my face to his, his fingers tangling in the mess of my hair. My ponytail had come loose, and Gray pulled it apart. There were no gentle kisses this time. His lips moved over mine like a man starving of hunger devouring his last meal. With his lips on mine, Gray picked me up and carried me back into the house and back into his bedroom.

This time our lovemaking was frenzied, and when he pushed into me, pain was mixed with my pleasure. Gray was not a small man, in any sense, and our earlier session coupled with long disuse left my poor lady parts the very best kind of sore. Gray seemed to sense this and slowed until the pain subsided and I cried for him to move harder, faster. Gray obliged, and soon his cries mixed with mine as we came together. This time Gray collapsed on top of me, and I wrapped my arms and legs around him and held him close.

When I woke up, Gray kissed me long and hard, then pulled me against his chest and held me close. He was a drowning man, and I was his life raft. He peppered my face with kisses, then let go.

"I have to get up," he said quietly. "I'm going out to the barn to feed the animals. I'll be back in a bit. Towels in the bathroom are clean if you want to shower."

I nodded, then watched as he got up and pulled on his clothes. The muscles of his back moved under his skin, firm and sure. He was so fit for a man his age. It could only be from all the work he did to run his farm. I felt positively lumpy compared to him, and I was grateful the covers hid my body. It was not like I was fat. Carrying pots and supplies kept me from running to fat, but I cooked all day, which meant I ate all day. Well, not really ate, more like tasted, but working around food did not keep me thin.

I got up as soon as Gray left the room and took a shower. He was still out in the barn when I got out, so I found my own clothes in the dryer and left the other woman's lying in a dirty laundry basket. I wasn't going to wear another woman's clothes again.

I was in the kitchen making breakfast for us when I heard a truck drive up. I stepped over to the kitchen door to see Gray and Justin unloading my tire from the back of my truck. He looked up as I stepped outside.

"Tire is changed, but this one's a loss," he said, then stuck his finger in a whole that marred the side of the rubber. "Weird blowout, too." He rolled the tire over and leaned it against his barn, and then he and Justin stepped into the kitchen.

"I made bacon-stuffed potato pancakes," I said as I set the table.

If Justin thought it was strange I was still there, he didn't say anything. He just tucked into my breakfast like the hungry young man he was.

"Chase is here," Gray said as another truck pulled into the farm. I moved to the stove to make another set of stuffed pancakes and had them on the table by the time Chase stepped into the kitchen.

"Can you stay all the time?" Justin asked through his mouthful.

"You wouldn't do anything but eat if she was here all the time," Gray joked, and Chase nodded, his own mouth full.

I cleaned up the kitchen, then wiped my hands on the towel.

"I should get back to the Spider," I said. "Is the road passable?"

Gray nodded and stood. "You should be OK," he answered. "But I can drive you if you want."

I shook my head, suddenly shy. "You've got enough to do. I'll be fine. Bye, guys," I called out and got waves from Justin and Chase. Then I walked over to my truck with Gray behind me.

"Claire," Gray said quietly, then pulled me over for a kiss. It was long and deep and made me want to turn around and go right back into his bedroom. Good grief, when had I turned into such a horndog?

"I'll see you later, OK?" he said, and I smiled and nodded, still basking in the glow of his kiss. I don't even remember the drive back to town or floating into the Spider where Luthien, Priss, and Mairen stared at me like I'd grown another head. Only Mairen's knowing smile brought me back down to earth.

"So how was your evening?" she asked, though I was pretty sure she knew perfectly well how my evening had gone.

"Fine," I answered. "I spent it soothing frightened goats." It was mostly true. "Were you guys OK here?" I asked to change the subject.

"We were fine," Mairen sang. "Some of the book club ladies showed up, but they just drank. Priss made flatbreads out of whatever was in the fridge, so everyone was happy, though maybe not quite as happy as you."

Priss snorted as she pushed off the barstool. "I'm going home to shower," she said. "I'll be back for lunch. We should be busy with people who got stuck by the storm."

Priss saluted us, then went out the door. Mairen and Luthien helped me unload the truck, and then they too set off for home now that the road was clear.

I went up to my apartment to change but stood at my living room window and stared off toward Gray's farm. I couldn't see the farm itself in the distance, but it was enough to be able to see the fields that marked the farthest edge of his property. Just thinking about him made me ache in parts that were already aching. I shook off my lust and went to put on some clean clothes.

Priss had been right when she said we'd be busy. Business was steady lunch through dinner, and we were just slowing down when Gray walked in. I'd been bored to tears listening to Jeff Smallings drone on and on about something or other. I seriously had no clue what he was yammering about since I had been daydreaming about Gray's lips.

I'll admit my heart skipped a beat. He looked the same, but everything about him had changed. I knew how he smelled when he lay on top of me, knew how he tasted. I knew the feel of his morning stubble against my naked breast. When he sat down at the bar in front of me, he gave me slow smile that made me want to tear off my clothes and climb on top of him.

Instead, I poured him a beer. When I slid it in front of him, his fingers laced through mine for a second and my heart thrilled.

"Let me get you a snack," I offered just to give myself a chance to get myself together and catch my breath. Priss and I had made garlic pretzel bites and spicy pralines so I grabbed bowls of both and set them in front of Gray.

"Thanks," he rumbled in his deep, rich voice. His fingers brushed mine again, then held them for a long moment before letting go.

I smiled, though it was a shaky smile, then moved off to help Luthien. Justin and Chase had come in and sat next to Gray, so I'd have an excuse to go back without looking like I just wanted to crawl into Gray's lap.

"I wanted to thank you for helping me with my tire," I said.

Embarrassed, Justin waved away my thanks, but Chase looked thoughtful.

"You know, I was looking at it again today, and it's really weird," he said slowly. "It looks more like a bullet hole than a blowout."

"You had a blowout?" Jeff asked from farther down the bar. Clearly, he'd been eavesdropping.

Gray turned and glared at him. "You were there, Smallings."

Jeff's brow furrowed, and he looked confused. "You mean last night? In the rain?" he asked, then gave me an awkward smile. "I thought you'd just had a breakdown. I didn't realize it was your tire."

Gray stared at him, then turned away without answering. "We'll have to drive over toward Cody to replace your spare. I don't want you stuck in case it happens again." Gray's eyes cut over to Jeff, who looked away.

This whole conversation was really weird, and I had no idea what to do with it. So I did nothing. I had a bar to run and wasn't interested in whatever existed between Jeff and Gray. It didn't have anything to do with me, and in my book, Gray would win every time.

Both men seemed to get the hint. Jeff moved off to regale a table full of women with his nonsense, and Gray settled in with Justin and Chase to talk farm talk while I stepped into the kitchen to help Priss clean up.

As much as I wanted to spend the night with Gray at the bar, the Spider was still a business, my business, and I was busy until closing. Gray had left earlier, and I was sorry I didn't get a nice, long good night kiss, but I understood. I said good-bye to Priss and the Ross kids, then locked up behind them. I debated driving over to Gray's as I made my way upstairs, but we weren't really at that point where I could just show up unannounced. I had just locked my door behind me when a pair of arms pulled me into the dark.

"Thank God," Gray whispered, then pressed his lips to mine. "I thought that bar would never close."

This is heaven, I thought as I pulled Gray close. Despite how tired I had been earlier, my body needed his. Still kissing, we moved to my bedroom and fell onto the bed. Gray undressed me while I pulled at the button that fastened his jeans. Soon we were naked, and I lay back as Gray's tongue wandered every inch of my body, his hands cupping my breasts, tickling the soft skin on the underside. Eventually his tongue found its way between my legs, and I cried out as it moved slowly along the length of my clitoris. I had been aching for him all night, so my orgasm began almost immediately. His fingers entered me as his tongue moved across the length of my clit, sending shivers through my body. A delicious itch built. Not wanting to come so fast, I held it off for as

long as I could, but Gray's tongue was masterful, and soon I was crying
out my pleasure. Suddenly Gray moved up and pressed himself against
me. I raised my legs and received the full length of him, smiling as he
cried out in his own pleasure. My orgasm began to build again, and we
shuddered as we came together. Gray's lips found mine, and his tongue
tasted of my salt.

When our hearts slowed, Gray moved away to draw the quilt over
us, then pulled me close against his chest. Soon we were both asleep.

SEVEN

I awoke to the early-morning light, cold and alone but not lonely. I knew Gray had to take care of his animals, so I lingered in bed, reveling in the aches and pains of a night of passion, then got up to start my day. On my small dining table, I found a note that just read *Come to the farm later*, and it was signed with a heart.

I smiled.

So this wasn't just a sex thing. Grown men didn't sign notes with hearts unless they meant it. At least I didn't think they did. Gray didn't seem like the type to sign a note with a heart regardless of how he felt about someone, but my note had a heart.

I took a shower and dressed, then sat in front of my computer to plan a menu that would keep me at Gray's for as long as possible. I finally settled on a goat cheese and tomato tarte with feta and spinach stuffed flank steak.

The kids were already in the bar when I went downstairs, and I swear they gave one another knowing looks when I mentioned the night's menu. To be honest, we had so much goat cheese in the fridge I could have just run to the market for everything else. Luckily, Priss threw me a bone and suggested cucumber and chèvre croquettes for lunch, which would seriously demolish our goat cheese inventory, giving me a solid reason to go to Gray's. Mairen got in on the game and suggested baked apples stuffed with goat cheese for dessert, and I wanted to kiss her. I said my farewells and left my crew to take care of the Spider in my absence.

Gray was outside in the pen with Chase while Justin manned the produce stand. With a smile, he took my list and filled my order while I wandered over to watch Gray and Chase. It looked like they were building a large wooden pyramid and were mostly done. Chase walked over to let me into the pen while Gray hammered the last board into place. He was shirtless, and I'm not ashamed to say I got a little flushed just looking at him. Chase went over to the barn and opened the door to the pen, then stood back as goats streamed past him. A dozen came my way to nudge my hand and bleat their greetings.

I waded my way through friendly bodies to where Gray stood, sweating in the sun.

I wanted to lick him.

"So what's this for?" I asked instead.

Gray tossed his hammer into the toolbox, then grabbed his T-shirt.

"Goats need something to play with or they get into trouble. Chase and I built them a jungle gym," he answered, then pulled me back as a crowd of goats moved over to inspect their new toy. "Watch."

Gray and I stood back as the goats inspected the new addition to their pen. At first, they were suspicious, and then one brave soul took the first step and jumped to the top. She bleated as if proud of her accomplishment, which prompted the others to follow. Soon the pyramid was covered and bore a striking resemblance to a Christmas tree, if Christmas trees were covered with goats.

"That's amazing." I laughed, and Gray laughed with me. Careful not to cover me with sweat, Gray pulled me next to him and gave me a kiss. When he moved back, I pressed my lips to his naked chest and kissed him just above his nipple. And, yes, I licked him.

"Lord, Claire, don't do that, or I'll have to throw you down into the dirt," he said, his voice low. I couldn't help but smile and notice that the front of his jeans had tented.

Gray picked up the toolbox and took my hand, then led me over to the barn where he stored the toolbox.

"Let me show you where our new chickens are going, so I can distract myself from wanting to tear those clothes off and throw you up into the hay loft."

I laughed and followed him out. We walked to a small building near the greenhouses where a handful of chickens pecked at the ground in front of them. Instead of talking about chickens, though, Gray took my face in his hands and kissed me. I could taste the salt of his sweat on him, and it was delicious. His tongue teased mine, and then he let me go and took my hand.

"I know it's Friday and you're busy tonight, but I'd really like you to spend the night here tonight instead of at the Spider," he said, his voice low but his gaze intense.

I couldn't find my voice, so I just nodded. He smiled in return, and I stared at the dimple next to his mouth like it was the most beautiful thing in the world. In a way it was. I'd seen Gray smile before, but I'd never seen that dimple. It was like it was mine alone, just for me.

Gray wrapped his arm around me, and I curled into his embrace, not caring if I got covered in his sweat. We walked back to my truck as Justin and Chase deliberately ignored our affection. Justin was all smiles though as I drove off.

I was on cloud nine when I got back to the Spider. Priss and I got lunch together, then worked to prep for dinner. Business was steady and we were busy even after the dinner crowd had left. I was still busing tables when Gray came in with Teddy. He took his regular seat at the bar and gave me a smile. Jeff Smallings showed up a little bit later and parked himself next to Gray, much to my annoyance. I gave Gray as much attention as I dared without setting off the town gossips, then closed up with Gray still sitting at the bar. Jeff Smallings was the last to leave, as if reluctant to do so until Luthien ushered him to the door. Mairen and Luthien said good night, followed by a smirking Priss. I locked up, then rode with Gray back to the farm.

It was late, and we both were tired. We settled on the couch, where I dozed in his arms, each breath filled with the scent of warm skin. I heard his heart beating against my cheek and felt mine beat in time. I was just on the edge of sleep when I felt the briefest brush of his lips against mine, then a second kiss, soft but firmer. My lips opened to his, and I felt his hand against my cheek, his fingers cradling me as his kiss deepened. When he pulled away, I opened my eyes to see him gazing at me intently. I returned his gaze, then opened the blanket to cover us as he pulled me onto his lap. Our lips met again with burning intensity. The touch of his tongue to mine sent a searing heat throughout my body. My tongue met his, and I smiled as his breath caught. A moment later he stood, lifting me in his arms, and carried me into the bedroom where he laid me gently on the bed. I wasn't interested in gentle, though. I pulled him on top of me and gloried when his hands moved over my body. Somehow buttons and zippers were undone, and I found myself pressed against the heat of his naked flesh. I groaned as his lips moved down my chest to latch on to my nipple. I felt him hard against my leg, and I wanted nothing more than to feel him inside me. Instead his fingers trailed up my inner thigh. The moment they touched me I was lost. It had been a long night of thinking about him, and his fingers were so skilled I was cresting the wave of orgasm in moments.

"Now," I panted.

He didn't need any more encouragement. Gray moved over me, then gently placed himself between my legs. When I realized how big he truly was, I was grateful for his patience. I reached down and wrapped my fingers around the length of him. He groaned as if waiting another second was agony, so I guided him inside me.

Oh my God.

This was how I want to die. With Gray inside me. He might not love me, but he wanted me, and maybe that was enough.

EIGHT

So Gray and I were a couple. Everyone quietly accepted our couplehood with the exception of Jeff Smallings, who was too dense to notice that Gray and I were together. It was kind of weird how competitive he was over someone who wasn't even remotely interested in him. One nice thing was that it seemed to humble him, and he wasn't trying so hard to impress, which made him kind of a nice guy. If he'd been this nice in the beginning, I might have been interested.

Well, that's not exactly true. Jeff was good-looking, but there had always been something about Gray that made my heart flutter, and other things flutter, too.

We had taken to spending so much time together that half of my clothes were at his house, so I'd invited Priss to stay in my apartment. She was happy to be closer to work, and I was happy to have someone there.

Gray and I fell into a pattern that meant lots of work, sex, and very little sleep. Since Mondays and Tuesdays were my slow days at the bar, Gray changed his schedule to reflect mine, and we rested on those days. We would get up together, eat, then go out and take care of the animals. Gray gave me easy jobs like feeding and harvesting produce while he and the boys took care of milking. He did teach me the fine art of cheese making, and I had a blast coming up with different flavors of cheeses, which I would test out at the Spider. In the evenings, he would come to the Spider and sit at the bar until closing, and then we'd go home, make love, then sleep.

I'd never been more tired or happier in my life.

We were closing in on four months of bliss when Gray hit me with a bombshell. We were having breakfast after feeding the animals when he made his announcement at the breakfast table.

"So I need to go back to Maryland for a few days," he said to the table. Justin and Chase looked up, then looked at each other.

"Is something wrong?" I asked, but in my bliss, it was really just an idle question. I knew he still owned his house back east and assumed his trip had something to do with that.

"No, just some stuff to take care of," he said, then got up and gave me a kiss. "I'm going to get some stuff together. Then I'll drop you off at the Spider."

"You're going today?" I asked, and Gray nodded.

It seemed kind of sudden. Not like, *Oh, by the way, I'm thinking about heading back east sometime soon.* He was leaving that day. Maybe even that hour. I wondered if something was wrong, then wondered where I should stay while he was gone. I didn't really feel comfortable being at the farm without him. It wasn't really my home, so I followed him into the bedroom and got my own clothes together.

Gray paused in his packing and looked at me. "What are you doing?"

"I don't feel right staying here without you, so I'll just go back to the Spider and stay there until you get back," I answered. "Besides, I don't trust myself driving back and forth so late at night."

Gray considered this, then nodded. He didn't resume packing, though, but moved over and pulled me close. "Don't take too much, though," he said, his voice low. "I want you back here when I get home."

I smiled and nodded, my heart aching with love for him. We'd never said the words, and it was killing me. I wanted to tell him I loved him, but I was afraid my love might not be reciprocated. I knew he had feelings for me, but he'd never articulated them, and for whatever reason, I didn't want to be the one to say them first.

We finished packing in silence, and then he drove me back to my bar. He kissed me good-bye, then drove off, leaving me to stare after him, wondering if I should have mustered the courage to tell him how I felt.

I let myself into the kitchen to find Priss cleaning the stove.

"So it looks like we'll be roomies for a bit," I said, trying to sound cheerful. "Gray has to go on a trip for a while, so I figured I'll stay here until he gets back."

Priss nodded, nonchalant. "Cool," she answered. "I'm going to finish this grill, then clean out the fridge."

I returned her nod. "OK. Let me drop this off upstairs, and I'll help."

I dragged my duffel up the stairs and into my room where I dropped it onto my bed. Priss had taken up residence in the smaller bedroom, but the apartment was so neat, it looked like she'd never stepped foot inside. I returned to the kitchen and started cleaning.

Gray's few days turned into a couple of weeks. He called every night and texted throughout the day, but his absence was incredibly painful. I'd grown so accustomed to being with him that my body ached for his. It was a biological imperative that he return to me or I would die of lust.

Finally, he sent me a text that he was expecting to return that Friday morning, and I was beside myself with excitement. I floated through lunch and dinner that night, wondering if I should spend the night at the farm so I would be there when he got back or just see him the next day. My fatigue won out, and I fell into my own bed that night, resolving to go over there first thing in the morning.

The next morning I was antsy to leave. Priss and I made our menu for the day so I would at least show up with a purpose and not look like some total loser pining for her man. I practically flew down the road in my truck, my smile so big it was starting to hurt my face.

I pulled up to the produce stand where Justin waited.

"Hey, Justin," I called out as I climbed out of my truck. He returned my greeting but looked profoundly uncomfortable. I was about to ask him what was wrong when the door to the house opened. I moved toward the house but stopped short when a tall, leggy blonde stepped out, followed by Gray.

I stared as she walked over to where I stood, openmouthed and in shock. She was wearing the pink flannel shirt and jeans I'd worn my first night at the farm, and they fit her perfectly. Everything fit her perfectly. Even her ponytail was perfect.

"You must be Claire," she said in a rich, low voice. "I'm Jennifer. Gray's wife."

And everything just went blank. When I say I don't remember what happened next, I'm not exaggerating. All I know is I turned away from the woman Gray was married to, got back into my truck, and drove away. It wasn't until I was miles and miles past Hester that I realized what had just happened. I was in the middle of nowhere, and my heart was breaking. I pulled into the parking lot of an old, abandoned gas station and quickly got out. I felt like I was going to be sick. I bent over and retched, but nothing came out. Tears burned my eyes, and my cries came out choking. I couldn't catch my breath. I couldn't speak. I couldn't do anything but stare at the gravel drive below my feet and wish for it to stop hurting. But it would never stop hurting. Gray was married and not to me. Gray had a wife, and it wasn't me. Gray had never told me he loved me, and now I knew why. Why would he love me when he had *her* for a wife?

More than anything, I wanted to pack everything up and drive away. I'd done it once before. Why not do it again? I entertained the thought for a solid minute, then discarded it. I didn't have anything before, but things were different now. I had the Spider and Priss and the Ross kids. I had friends. I didn't have anything to leave before, but I did now. Now I had too much to leave. I stood and stared off into the distance and waited until the pain turned to a numb ache, and then I got into my truck, turned around, and drove back to Hester.

Gray's truck waited for me at the Spider, and as soon as I spotted it, tears burned my eyes. Gray stepped out as soon as I parked, but I was in no mood to talk to him.

"Claire," he said, his tone beseeching.

"I don't want to talk to you," I replied. I sounded as dead as I felt. I pushed past him toward the door, but he caught my hand.

"I need to explain, Claire. It's not what you think."

I turned back and looked at him. I loved him so much, and it was killing me.

"Are you married to her?" I asked.

Gray dropped my hand and looked away. It was all the answer I needed.

I turned and went into the Spider, letting the door slam behind me.

I tried to make light of the situation, but it was hard. Everyone in town knew what had happened, and it didn't help that Luthien, Mairen, and even Priss were treating me like I might shatter at any minute. Priss kept me in the kitchen or Luthien kept me behind the bar as if they could protect me from the hurt that came with every sad smile or kind word. The only person who seemed happy was Jeff Smallings, who acted like the world was his oyster.

When the dinner rush was finally over, Luthien gave me the task of washing every glass in the bar, even ones that weren't dirty. It was busywork, but I was grateful for it. It kept me from having to answer uncomfortable questions. With my back to the room, I couldn't see the pitying looks people kept sending my way. Unfortunately, I couldn't see the door, either, and it wasn't until a shocked hush moved through the room that I realized something had happened. That something was Gray walking in, followed by his wife.

I stood and stared at them. Unbelievable. This was my home, my business. How dare he come in here, and how dare he bring her with him? So what if he'd turned and snapped at her like she wasn't welcome. She got here somehow, didn't she? She was living in his house. How could he not know she would walk in with him?

Gray moved to his regular seat at the bar but didn't sit. Instead, he stood and quietly called my name. To his credit, he looked uncomfortable. His wife didn't share his discomfort, though, and made herself at home on the next barstool. I could feel the space behind my eyes swell with rage. I wanted to scream at them to get out. Instead I turned and walked straight into the kitchen, my face burning. Priss looked up, startled, then glanced through the open door behind me. Her face turned to a scowl, and she moved quickly to shut the door.

"Go upstairs," Priss said gently, moving me toward my apartment door. "We got this."

And I knew they did. I went upstairs and stood in the middle of my living room, completely drained. The rage had left me as soon as the door had closed behind me, and I welcomed the numbness that took its place. I was contemplating my next move when I heard noises outside. I stepped to my living room window and looked down to see Gray arguing with someone on the sidewalk. It looked like Margaret, and it looked like she was telling him to leave with Teddy standing between them as referee. Gray's wife stood nearby with her hands across her chest, a small smile on her face. Gray and Margaret starting yelling at each other, and my eyes began to burn. I couldn't really hear what they were saying, and it didn't matter. Gray's wife stood by like she had a right to be there, and I supposed she did.

Suddenly Gray looked up, and I quickly stepped away from the window. I knew he couldn't see me through the blinds, but I still didn't want to give him the satisfaction of knowing how much he hurt me or how much I still cared. I waited a moment, then glanced out again, but everyone was gone. A part of me wanted Gray to storm the bar to get to me, yet another part knew it was pointless. No matter what he did, his wife would be standing over his shoulder, smiling her beautiful little smile.

NINE

I stopped going to Gray's farm. If we needed anything from there, either Priss went to get it or someone delivered it. I suspected that someone was Gray, but Luthien or Priss accepted the deliveries without saying a word about who had dropped it off.

Thankfully, whatever Margaret had said to Gray kept him away, and everyone made a concerted effort to avoid any conversation about Mr. and Mrs. Childs. I had no idea what had happened with them, and I wanted to keep it that way. I stopped paying attention to just about everyone unless they were speaking directly to me, and even then, it was an effort to focus on what they were saying. The only person who didn't seem to mind was Jeff. He'd made Gray's usual seat his own and spent most nights chattering at me like a monkey. He'd stopped glad-handing the bar, though, and his conversations were sometimes, if not interesting, somewhat amusing. He'd been speculating on the possibility of farming his land or raising animals when I noticed that he didn't seem like such a dick. Luthien stood nearby, drying glasses and making suggestions.

"I wouldn't do rabbits," Luthien stated gravely. "People ranch for food or wool, and they're way too cute to eat. Chickens aren't cute. What about chickens?"

"I was thinking alpacas," Jeff countered. Any other time he would have sounded like an idiot, but tonight he sounded thoughtful. "I've read they're great for wool. And they're not that cute if someone wants to eat one."

I surprised myself by laughing, and the way everyone jumped, I must have surprised them, too, though they began to laugh with me.

When the hilarity died down, I noticed Jeff was watching me closely but with a kind smile. He seemed like he was worried about me, and it felt good to know someone cared.

"So I was wondering if you'd like to come see my new farm set up," he said quietly. "I know we're joking about my raising animals, but I've actually been working on bringing in alpacas. I have a guy dropping off a small herd next week."

It was a nice invitation, and Jeff seemed sincere. I considered it for a second, but in my heart, it just didn't seem right.

"I'm not really ready to date right now," I answered and felt horrible when his face fell.

"It's not meant to be a date," he countered, then softened the sharp remark with a smile. "Just giving you a reason to get out of the Spider, get some fresh air."

I thought about that. I'd been avoiding the world as much as possible, so I hadn't left the Spider in almost a month. Why not? It was not like he was asking me on a date.

"OK," I said with a shrug. "Sure."

Jeff gave me a sweet smile, and I felt better for having said yes. At least he wasn't married. Or was he? It didn't really matter. I wasn't going to date him. I moved off to help Luthien, leaving a smiling Jeff sitting at the bar.

Jeff pestered me for the next week so that Saturday I drove out to his property to see what he was so excited about. I saw Gray's farm off in the distance, but I avoided looking at it. Instead I focused on the man standing in front of me. Jeff waved from the porch, the bright blue of his button-down setting off his tan face nicely. I marveled at the tan. Jeff didn't seem like the kind of guy to spend a lot of time outside unless it was golfing. I wondered if he had a tanning bed, then shook off the thought. It didn't really matter anyway.

I smiled as Jeff stepped off the porch and gave me an awkward kiss on the cheek. We made desultory conversation as he led me to a pen filled with long-necked furry creatures I assumed were the alpacas. I'd never actually seen one before. They looked like small llamas and seemed friendly though a little nervous around us. I wondered if Jeff ever petted them or if he just liked having them around like it some-how completed the image of a Wyoming rancher. I glanced at Jeff, who looked very clean for having entered alpaca ranching. I admired his alpacas, then the alpaca barn, then made moves to leave.

"Oh, I was hoping you'd stay a little longer," he said. "I made us some lunch."

I hadn't really planned on eating lunch with him but oh well. He'd gone to the trouble of putting together a meal.

"Thanks." I followed Jeff into the house, then took a moment to take it all in. From the outside it looked like a large but modest ranch house, but inside it was like stepping into a five-star mountain lodge. The furnishings looked expensive, and Jeff had clearly hired a decorator to give the home that perfect Wyoming touch.

"Your home is very nice." And it was, if a little overdone.

Jeff smiled. "Thanks. It's cozy." Not the word I would have used but...whatever.

He led me to a table laden with meats and cheeses with warm-baked bread. A tossed salad sat nearby with a bottle of white wine chilling in an ice bucket.

"Uh...this isn't quite what I was expecting."

Jeff smiled again like it was a compliment, then pulled out a chair for me. I sat and let him serve me as he chatted about his first effort at buying livestock. I know it was meant to be funny, but I just couldn't shake the feeling that Gray was just across the field. I tried to put him out of my mind, but it was impossible when he was so close.

"You know we would have a much nicer time if you'd stop mooning over Grayson Childs."

I startled out of my daydream, feeling both guilty and annoyed. Jeff looked angry and pompous, like the old glad-handing big talker Jeff.

"I should go," I said, then got up to leave.

"No, don't go," Jeff snapped. "At least have some wine. I had it shipped all the way from Napa."

I was starting to feel uncomfortable, but he had a right to be upset. He'd gone to a lot of trouble. I took a sip of the wine. It was very cold and overly sweet, but Jeff looked so hopeful that I took another long sip, then selected one of the cheeses from the cheese board. I was raising it to take a bite when my hand dropped to my lap. What was wrong with me? The world had gone a little blurry around the edges. I couldn't feel my lips anymore, and my head was dropping no matter how hard I tried to lift it.

When my eyes opened again, it was still light. I still couldn't move, but I was awake. I heard voices in the other room, then in my fog wondered how they were in the other room. What room was I in? I tried to move my head, but I could only press it farther into the bed.

Bed?

How did I end up on a bed? With herculean effort I raised my eyes to look toward the window. It was open, and a light breeze blew across my naked skin, raising goosebumps across my flesh.

Oh my God. I was naked...in Jeff Smallings bed. Oh my God. How did I get here?

"What do you want, Smallings?" a voice asked. It sounded like Gray. I tried to call out, but nothing was working right. "Why is Claire's truck here?" he asked.

"She's resting right now," Jeff answered.

Resting? "Resting?" Gray asked. "What are you talking about?"

I heard a door open behind me.

"Claire?" It was Gray, and I couldn't turn my head to ask him for help. I couldn't do anything.

"I told you she's resting," Jeff said, his voice low.

"Claire." It sounded like an order, and I knew Gray wasn't convinced. I heard him move around the bed, then saw him move into the space in front of me. Jeff was protesting, but I stopped listening to him. I needed Gray to understand me.

"Grrraa," was all I could get out.

"Claire?" Gray whispered and put his hand on the side of my face. I closed my eyes and let the tears fall. At least they still worked.

"Let her sleep, Gray." Jeff was still trying to convince Gray I was there voluntarily.

Gray stood, and I already missed his face. He pulled his phone out of his pocket.

"Justin, grab Chase and come on over to Smallings place right now," I heard him say. Somewhere near the door, Jeff started to protest, but Gray ignored him.

"This is Gray Childs. I need an ambulance at Smallings farm off Route 14. I'm not sure. It seems like a drug poisoning. Send the sheriff."

Gray knelt next to me and placed his hand on the side of my face. He spoke softly and dried my tears with his thumb.

"I don't know what he did to you, but I'm going to get you out of here."

I tried to press my face into his hand, but I still couldn't move.

"Boss?" I heard behind me, and Gray moved to pull the blanket over me. "Miss Claire?"

"Watch Smallings," Gray ordered. "Claire's been drugged."

There was a scuffle behind me, and in the distance, I could hear the wail of a siren. Gray stayed with me as the paramedics came in to examine me. Another siren approached and grew louder until it abruptly cut off. Things were getting very gray around the edges. I could hear Gray calling for me, but he sounded so far away. Why was he so far away?

"Claire? Claire..."

TEN

I woke up in the hospital to an IV in my arm and an empty room, but I could move. The world still felt fuzzy and strange. I turned my head to see Gray out the window talking to a sheriff's deputy. He glanced at me, then, when he saw I was awake, hurried into my room.

"Oh my God, Claire." He rushed to my bed and knelt next to me, his hand going to the side of my face. "You're awake."

"What happened?" I whispered. I only had a vague idea of what was going on.

"Smallings gave you some kind of drug. The doctors think it was ketamine."

"Why?" I'd said it quietly, but I was screaming it in my head.

Gray shook his head. "I don't know. They did a rape kit, and it came back negative. I think he just wanted me to see you like that. Like you and he had..." Gray paused and shook his head.

"But why would he want that? Why would that matter?"

Gray's eyes searched mine. "Because you're mine, Claire. Because I love you. I love you so much...and you love me, and he didn't want that."

It was what I'd always wanted to hear, but it didn't matter anymore. I shook my head as tears fell and turned away.

"Don't, Claire. Don't cry. Why are you crying?"

"Because I'm not yours. Someone else is."

"No, Claire," Gray replied and turned my face to his. "You were mine the minute you climbed into that goat pen. Jennifer would never have done that. She wouldn't even have been here if I hadn't admitted to our relationship. She left me a long time ago. I went back to Maryland to make her sign the divorce papers, but she got wind of you and didn't like being replaced. So she came here to cause trouble for me...for us."

I searched Gray's eyes for the lie, but it wasn't there. He did love me. I raised my hand to touch those lips I'd missed so dearly, then dropped it.

"But you're still married."

Gray smiled and shook his head. "Nope. I filed for a no-fault divorce and accused her of adultery. Luckily, Jennifer's boyfriend was pissed she came out here and showed up to back me up. The papers are filed."

And with that, a little spark of hope burst into flame. Maybe not the most conventional declaration of love, but I'd take it.

"What happens to Smallings?"

Gray's face grew serious. "He's been charged with possession and attempted sexual assault. They tested the wine, and it had been poisoned. He's going to prison."

Good, I thought. *May he rot there.*

Gray leaned over and pressed his lips to mine, and I forgot all about Jeff Smallings.

ELEVEN

Not all stories have happy endings, but this one does. Gray's divorce was final, but not without a few hiccups. Jennifer came back a couple of times to try to reconcile. But even to the casual observer, it was nothing but an attempt to maintain her lifestyle back in Maryland, which Gray had been funding. The second time, her boyfriend, Steve, followed her to Wyoming, which made her attempts to woo Gray back kind of entertaining.

He ate at the Spider a couple of times, and I found him to be perfectly nice, if a little deluded. He wanted to marry Jennifer, and I wished him the very best of luck with that one. She was more suited to someone like Jeff Smallings but had her claws sunk deep into poor Steve, who thought she walked on water.

Eventually Jennifer gave up, and Gray was able to fully sever his last tie to Maryland.

Speaking of Jeff, with overwhelming evidence that he'd poisoned my wine with a date rape drug but didn't actually rape me, he was given a plea deal. Of course he tried to negotiate it, then argue it, but eventually he pled guilty for a reduced sentence and was sent to prison. The cost of his defense sent him into near bankruptcy, and his land went into foreclosure. Gray bought the land and expanded his farm to include the poor, unfortunate alpacas, who flourished under his care. The house was turned into a retreat center and, with Mairen's help, was already doing well.

As for me, I'm still at the Spider with Luthien, Mairen, and Priss. We're thinking about expanding to Cody or Jackson Hole, but it would mean Priss leaving me, and I'm not sure I'm quite ready for that yet. Otherwise, business is great, and every day I thank my good fortune that my car broke down when it did.

Hester, Wyoming, is a wonderful town filled with wonderful people, and it's my home now.

Love,

Claire Childs

P.S. BTW, the wedding was beautiful.